VIRVE SAMMALKORPI

TRANSLATED FROM THE FINNISH
BY EMILY JEREMIAH AND
FLEUR JEREMIAH

Peirene

Paflagonian perilliset

AUTHOR

We celebrate Virve Sammalkorpi as one of the most powerful voices to emerge in Finnish literature for a generation. She published her first novel in 1999 and has written seven novels in total. Sammalkorpi's most recent novel, *Children of the Cave*, won both the 2017 Savonia Literature Prize and the Kuvastaja Prize for the best Finnish Fantasy Novel. This is the first time one of her books has been translated into English.

TRANSLATORS

Emily Jeremiah and Fleur Jeremiah form a multilingual mother-and-daughter translation team. Emily and Fleur have co-translated works by numerous Finnish poets and novelists. They are also the translators of Peirene No. 7, *The Brothers*, Peirene No. 11, *Mr Darwin's Gardener* and Peirene No. 16, *White Hunger*.

MEIKE ZIERVOGEL
PEIRENE PRESS

Greek legends, fables and fairy tales all share an interest in mythical beings. In this book Sammalkorpi imagines what would happen if these creatures really existed. How would we respond? The answer to this question matters hugely. It determines what it means to be human.

First published in Great Britain in 2019 by
Peirene Press Ltd
17 Cheverton Road
London N19 3BB
www.peirenepress.com

First published under the original Finnish-language title *Paflagonian perilliset*

ISBN 978-1-908670-50-2

Designed by Sacha Davison Lunt
Photographic Images: Filip Fuxa / 123RF
Typeset by Tetragon, London
Printed and bound by T J International, Padstow, Cornwall

This work has been published with the financial assistance of FILI – Finnish Literature Exchange.

FILI
FINNISH LITERATURE EXCHANGE

VIRVE SAMMALKORPI

TRANSLATED FROM THE FINNISH
BY EMILY JEREMIAH AND
FLEUR JEREMIAH

Peirene

Children
of the Cave

Preface

This story is a tribute to a man whose life is little known. He never became a great scientist or explorer. But he did preserve a small collection of images for future generations, thereby making his modest mark on a century of major inventions.

Iax Agolasky was born in Russia in 1795, the only child of Marushka and Vladimir Agolasky. Vladimir, his father, was a scholar and a polyglot. In addition to his native Russian, Iax learned French from his father. Iax gradually became interested in France, that distant land, seeing its language as his second mother tongue. He emigrated there as a young man.

In Paris, the young Iax managed to secure a position as an assistant at the Académie des Sciences. At the age of twenty-two, he was asked to act as assistant and interpreter to one Professor Moltique on an expedition to north-west Russia.

Professor Jean Moltique was a proponent of an early branch of anthropology that researched ancient peoples by means of folklore and legends. He was rumoured to have discovered the footprints of a yeti, possibly even an actual yeti, though none could prove this achievement. The journey undertaken by Professor Moltique and Agolasky lasted from 1819 to 1823, at least. Partly because of defective documentation, partly because of missing notes, no one knows exactly where Agolasky and Moltique travelled.

A letter written by Moltique to the Académie des Sciences reveals that he and Agolasky discovered a small tribe of forest dwellers in the wilderness. Moltique dubbed the members of this tribe *les enfants des ombres*, the children of shadows. He had at first taken these forest dwellers to be descendants of the ancient Anatolian people of Paphlagonia, but he changed his mind in the course of the expedition. In the words of the professor, his new theory was 'audacious and unprecedented'. The letter in which these words appear was filed in the academy's archives without any associated reports or memoranda. No one knows, therefore, what sentiments or proposals for action it may have prompted among academicians.

Much of the expedition remains shrouded in mystery. The first and only news reports concerning it date back to 1823, when Professor Moltique and Iax Agolasky returned from their Expedition of All Times, as the press referred to the trip. The fuss soon subsided. Without the surviving pages of Iax Agolasky's diary, the venture would have been permanently overshadowed by more significant feats performed in a century now famed for its great inventions and innovations. The names Moltique and Agolasky are nevertheless worth remembering. Every discovery needs numerous dreamers and adventurers behind it: to experiment, to err – and to show the way to others who may yet prove wiser and more fortunate.

It is my hope that I shall see something that nobody has ever before witnessed – and record my tale for future generations. That would mean that I could die happy.

—IAX AGOLASKY IN HIS LETTER TO PROFESSOR MOLTIQUE APPLYING TO BECOME THE LATTER'S ASSISTANT

These are the only entries surviving from the beginning of the diary. They do not throw much light on the initial stages of the expedition, but they indicate that Agolasky and Moltique's journey to north-west Russia had begun.

MAY 15TH IN THE YEAR 1819

– even when I left home. I am grateful to Moltique for selecting me from among the dozens of those who applied, all keen to go on this exciting journey. He was of course known to me, given his association with countless incredible-sounding adventures. There are those who allege that he owes his career to his connections and inheritance, but such claims can be put down to sour grapes. I gather he is also esteemed – though he is known for his coarse conduct, too, as well as for his public criticism of Church doctrine relating to the immortality of the soul.

My yearning to travel conquers all my prejudices.

Our journey has commenced, and I cannot get to sleep at night, my agitation is so –

JUNE – IN THE YEAR 1819

Mon Dieu, I never thought I would see –

– were far more impressive than I ever imagined –

I wonder what tomorrow will bring.

We may assume that the party travelled more or less directly through Europe to the Russian border. There is nothing to indicate that Moltique harboured any particular enthusiasm for this leg of the journey or that he had any objectives relating to it. He was probably in a hurry to find the descendants of the Paphlagonians. Diary entries resume from the day the camp was set up in north-west Russia; the notes give no more accurate geographical location.

UNDATED

– a narrow but torrential river runs through the coniferous forest. The site is ideal for our camp. We erected the tents and our men began to build a simple log cabin, to be used for storing goods and, when it gets colder in late autumn, for shelter. The horses will also need a stable.

We constructed a small store for provisions to which a ladder grants access, for we do not want uninvited animal guests there, or in any part of the camp. I have seen a wolverine, a fox, deer, elks, hares and assorted wildfowl in the forest nearby, and have resolved to benefit from our assistants' expertise in the matters of forest fauna and hunting. My father was never drawn to these matters and consequently never acquainted me with the wonders of the woods, preferring to lure me to the books in his library.

We established a place for a fire in front of the cabin and the tents, and will later build a shelter close by where we may eat in comfort. Our lavatory is just a plank at a fair distance from the camp. I would have wanted it even further away, but, as it seemed our assistants found even the present location hard to reach before dropping their trousers, I agreed to this spot, within shouting distance of the fire but out of sight, behind some rocks.

Jotted in the margin is a list of the provisions brought along by the expedition party:

Rice
Grain
Wine
Cognac
Absinthe
Cigars
Smoked, cured and salted meat
Dried fish, salt fish
Eggs
Raisins
Walnuts, hazelnuts and almonds
Dried herbs
Spices
Onions
Root vegetables
Fat
Beans
Olives
Tea
Sugar
Salt

We have set up our camp with care because, if the information Moltique has received is true, we shall be studying the mysterious forest tribe for a long time, perhaps even years. I am excited, believing that we shall find the tribe, even though its exist-ence is as improbable as that of the abominable snowman. Having heard the story of Moltique and the yeti, I asked him about it, but he merely snorted. He considers me young and inexperienced, I realized, resolving not to pry further. Instead, I went to set traps for hares. As long as we have not found the Paphlagonians' descendants, as we call the forest tribe of the tales, I have nothing to do but jot down our daily activities and the weather conditions. Moltique is most particular about some things, more casual about others, indifferent even. He has his own acerbic sense of humour and is cultured in many ways. I admire his scientific, unsentimental approach even though –

All the entries for May 1820 have been badly damaged, but the single lines that have been preserved indicate what a turning point the month represented for the expedition. Almost a year has passed since the beginning of the journey.

MAY 7TH IN THE YEAR 1820

This is a big day in the history of our expedition –

There are bones near the cave, along with other signs of life –

MAY 15TH IN THE YEAR 1820

It appears that we have discovered the habitat of a new animal species instead of a mysterious forest tribe. There are no signs of a human settlement.

MAY 22ND IN THE YEAR 1820

The animals of the cave appear mostly to move on two legs –

We do not know what animals they are. They appear quite small –

Moltique is greatly excited. He did not touch his food tonight, though we had not eaten all day, as we were looking for more traces –

MAY 25TH IN THE YEAR 1820

It rained in the morning, for all the day was warm. The rainfall ceased after lunch and the sun came out again – The wet ground was covered in prints.

MAY 28TH IN THE YEAR 1820

I think I was the first to see it –

I took it for a wild boar at first, but when the creature stood up I was certain for a moment that I was facing a human being. I had no time to give warning. A shot rang out.

MAY 30TH IN THE YEAR 1820

I did not tell Moltique, but the examination of the creature we felled gave me nightmares. The details I had noted down swirled in my mind: I dreamed of a human being with the ears of a cat, the muzzle of a dog, the tail of a pig, the hooves of a cow and the feathers of an owl –

A couple of longer extracts have fortunately survived from the entries for June 1820 and these give a better picture of the events that took place during the early stages of the expedition.

I know Moltique considers the creature we shot to be a monkey bearing unusual mutations. I myself cannot forget thinking I first saw a wild boar, then a human being. I do trust Moltique, and yet I wondered aloud what species of monkey lived in these latitudes, giving Moltique the opportunity to snort disparagingly. He pointed his pipe stem at me and asked if I had never before heard of the unheard-of.

I asked the professor what could have caused the strange mutations in the monkey, and he said, teasingly – knowing my religious upbringing – that the mutations were the work of Satan himself. I was taken aback by his mockery. Then he became serious and told me about countless other oddities he had seen while on his travels. The changes in the monkey are but one of the myriad wonders of the world, he implied. Several years have gone by since he last caused a stir in French scientific circles and I had the impression he was planning a Great Return. I hope he succeeds, for it would help me to get established as a recorder and chronicler in the service of notable explorers.

Moltique is not an easy taskmaster, but I can be thankful that I am able to be part of this adventure.

I have earlier told of May 7th, the day we found the cave, though I have not described our find in any detail. I come back to the subject because, as a child, I always dreamed of discovering a perfect cave with a sand-covered floor and a bubbling freshwater spring into which daylight filtered prettily. I have no way of knowing if this cave is like that inside; I imagine going inside one day, but I want to be on my own, without Moltique and our assistants. So far, we have only seen the exterior of the cave. Its low, humble mouth opens out into a pleasant, grassy field which enjoys sunlight from dawn to dusk. Now, in early summer, the grass is still green and vigorous, but later it will no doubt become burnt and dry. The opening is surrounded by a dense mixed forest dominated by spruces. The same narrow but torrential river that we use daily for our cooking and ablutions flows through it. The river water is translucent in the sunlight, like amber, revealing round stones, fine reddish gravel and graylings that rest close to the bottom – the men catch them for our meals. I am excited, marvelling at nature's cornucopia, and it becomes ever easier for me to understand how the man-like monkeys survive in this wilderness. It is hard, though, to imagine what winter will bring. I have never before lived out in the open in the middle of a forest.

JUNE 15TH IN THE YEAR 1820

In the morning, discussing our discovery, I asked what the professor now thought about our quest to find the Paphlagonians' descendants. He looked at me as if I were slow-witted and said that the nature of our expedition changed the day we shot our first monkey. He told me he had a new theory that he had not completely finalized but on which he was working daily. I was hoping he would enlighten me as to his hypothesis, but he sank back into his thoughts. Soon after breakfast, I got up and –

– our assistants told me that Moltique anticipates another hunting trip, once we have observed the cave and its inhabitants for long enough. He wants more detail as to what the creatures look like, their activities, their diet, how they procreate –

– there's no hurry. Moltique is prepared for this expedition to last years –

JUNE 21ST IN THE YEAR 1820

Moltique and I were ambling from the cave to the camp, just the two of us, and because, unusually, he happened to be in an expansive mood – indeed, I have often been the target of his arrogant, acid tongue – he kindly told me his preliminary thoughts, to the effect that mankind originally evolved from an animal state.

This revelation set my mind in turmoil. At home, I had become familiar with the doctrines of the Bible. But of course, as my father was a learned man, I had been brought up to be not just religious but also tolerant. Moltique got carried away by his ideas and lectured me during the whole journey through the forest. Only when we parted did I get the opportunity to ask myself a question: did Moltique mean to say that the cave dwellers were animals in the process of evolving into human beings? I would have liked him to explain further, but he did not appear at dinner. He merely sent a message to say he was concentrating on his work. I had his portion of wood grouse sent to the tent where –

– it is early morning and I will now stop writing my notes, though I know I shall not be able to sleep. I am in turmoil, given all I have heard, and oppressed by my ignorance.

JUNE 28TH IN THE YEAR 1820

Today we managed to approach the cave without the inhabitants spotting us. As we observed, they simply went about their business.

Cavorting on the grass in front of the cave, the creatures bore an uncanny resemblance to human children. In a fit of atypical lyricism, Moltique called them children of shadows. The name is apt, for they are prone to withdraw from direct light.

JULY, DATE ILLEGIBLE, IN THE YEAR 1820

– I thought Moltique's joke was unacceptably coarse, but our men guffawed loudly. They are like a pack of hounds that have acquired the taste of blood – We all suffer from a bottomless hunger all the time. Hunting is not only necessary, it also provides agreeable variety and excitement; life in the camp is monotonous. I myself have learned a great deal while accompanying Bruno, our hunter. The prey is stabbed, then the blood and superfluous innards are removed. This guarantees the preservation of the prey and the quality of the meat. Gutting requires supple fingers and precision. The dogs are rewarded with the innards we don't need – All this is part of our daily life. I respect and would like to thank all who keep us in food, but I did not like the joke that was directed at the small, slight creature close to the cave mouth –

Probably the first entire entry of the diary.

Assisting Moltique has granted me access to many
new experiences, as I have already indicated. My
diaries are unlikely to be of any great historical sig-
nificance, but they may well entertain other lovers
of distant lands, if published. I can imagine most
Parisians finding my description of the landlord of
that *Bierstube* amusing. Some of my tales hint at
the great upheavals that lie just ahead. During our
journey, we encountered a man from the United
Kingdom of the Netherlands who dreamed of
building a self-propelling carriage. He sounded perfectly sane, though I was not able to have a proper
conversation with him; Moltique was too busy
trumpeting his own achievements.

But in any case, Moltique has already led me to
places I could only dream of as a little boy. For a
long time, I thought I would live like my father, surrounded by books, far from the world about which
he taught me. Growing up, however, I began to feel
a pressing need to break away and to enter the life
my childhood in a learned home had been preparing
me for. So I moved to Paris. I still remember how I
felt, realizing that I was no longer being followed
by my father's stern but caring gaze or my mother's
loving eyes. The freedom I had dreamed of took my
breath away, almost crushing me. I wanted to crawl

under the bed like my dog, Noir, who was afraid
of thunder. I spent most of the first week in Paris
in my room, barely bold enough to buy bread from
the bakery downstairs. Then I decided to spread my
wings and enjoy my freedom.

I thought of the past today, walking back to the
camp from the cave, having been to observe the children going about their morning activities. I stayed
behind trees, but some of them clearly sensed –
smelt? – my presence and withdrew into the cave.
It was the fear that I discerned in the children that
prompted me to recall my departure from home
and my first days in Paris, filled as these were with
a mixture of joy and terror. I wonder why they are
not able to enjoy their life of freedom amid nature.
They appear to observe the surrounding forest con-
stantly, as if expecting to be taken away. Or perhaps
they do so hopefully, not fearfully? The smallest
and most animal-like of them cavorted with abandon just by the mouth of the cave. I have never seen
them glancing into the distance or watching their
backs in the same way as the older children.

Today, I paid attention to a girl who looked
smaller than many of the children but who is clearly
respected by them. She seemed to be in charge of
organizing the group's daily activities, albeit in her
own unsystematic way. I saw her carry something
edible to a large leaf in the grassy clearing where the
children assembled upon waking in the mornings
and then again in the evenings before retreating into
the cave to sleep. Because not all the children are
equally sociable, I tried to memorize those whom

I saw today. I recognized a tall, fair boy whose back is covered by dense, blond fur, and another whose large, rodent-like ears I have spied only with the help of my telescope. I cannot distinguish the animal feature of the slender girl from my hiding place – I wonder if Moltique is on the wrong track, after all. As I have already mentioned, we long ago buried his original theory of the children being the descendants of the Paphlagonians as fundamentally shaky and unfounded.

According to the professor's new theory, the children represent an intermediate stage in human evolution. I have heard that similar arguments have been proposed in more radical scientific circles, but no one has any evidence to support them. Despite my religious upbringing and irrespective of the fact that Moltique does not have a background as a natural scientist, I have until now been inclined to believe that there is a vestige of truth in his theory. Perhaps man and animals could have evolved from the same original species. Perhaps the children of the cave do represent an in-between stage in this process, or then they have developed their animal features out of necessity. As for the latter hypothesis, I have heard talk in Paris; there are those who are convinced that acquired characteristics can be inherited by the next generation. If the children of the cave were related, they should, as far as I can see, share similar characteristics. They do not all look the same. What about the girl who appears fully human to me? No, no, no. Something about what I saw today makes me doubt Moltique's theory. This worries me. I ask myself: if I do not believe in Moltique's theory, what do I believe in? I was taught that God created man in His own image. But all of us under this heavenly vault are God's creatures.

I would love to have a companion to talk to. I will think about all this and return to the topic later.

An addendum to the day's entry: it is night-time and Moltique has retreated into his tent, his summer accommodation. I have only just come back from a late-night walk to the cave. It was quiet there and I suspected that the children were already asleep. On my way back through the summery, moonlit forest I heard rustling in the bushes and the grass. I thought I heard a whispering that sounded very much like human speech – it could even have been my mother tongue, Russian – but because at the same time I saw eyes glinting in the dark, I expect I was wrong. Looks like I drank too much of the wine and cognac Moltique kept offering me during the meal. I just have to believe that the children are not human beings but a hybrid form of life between man and beast. I have seen it with my own eyes. God is great and His ways are mysterious. Father, can I rely on this single truth I know?

JULY 15TH IN THE YEAR 1820

I happened to come to the cave when the slender girl was alone in the grassy clearing, to the right of the mouth of the cave. I secretly called her Petite

('small' in French) in my mind, though I should
not name the creatures, for they are research
subjects. I examined her from a distance and tried
to work out what she was doing. It was a shame I
had left the telescope at the camp. It looked as if
Petite were doing embroidery, the way my mother
did, but I understood this was not possible, given
Moltique's theory and the habitat: how could a
creature representing an intermediate stage between
animal and human handle such intricate manual
manoeuvres? And what equipment would she use?
Presumably the girl was busy with something else,
though I could not see what the white material was
that she had on her knees. Perhaps a piece of skin
from which she was removing hairs. We have noted
that a proportion of the children cover themselves
in skins and skirt-like garments which they weave
from grass. We have not been able to establish
the origins of the materials used in the clothing.
According to Moltique, animals do not cover
themselves but deploy simple aids as necessary.
During his numerous expeditions he has observed
monkeys, among other specimens, and I am familiar with his notes about them. Of the simple attire
worn by the children of the cave, he has remarked
only that their need to clothe themselves is perhaps
their most human trait. He sees no contradiction in
commenting in a similar way on (other) animals. I
find it difficult to criticize his views, for I am painfully aware of my lack of sufficient knowledge of
science concerning man, nature and life in general.
My character and education make me more of a

philologist and a collector of tales. I dream not
so much of solving the mystery of life as of the
immortality of ideas.

The other night Moltique and I had a discussion about whether the children of the cave were
more human than animal. On the basis of their
behaviour, traits and habitat, Moltique regards
them primarily as animals. Our discussion led us
to moral and ethical considerations about what
was permissible and acceptable as far as research-
ing the children was concerned, assuming they are
animals. Moltique pointed at me with the bone he
was gnawing and asked if I thought it was appropri-
ate to eat hare. Would I prefer to eat him instead?
he queried. I in turn asked why we call the children
of the cave *children*, not *cubs* or *whelps*, which
would be more natural if they really were animals.
I explained that my remarks were based purely on
my background as a philologist and that I understood that they did not in themselves overturn or
even weaken Moltique's theory, but that I was afraid
our choice of words revealed that in our hearts we
considered the occupants of the cave human beings.
I felt it would be tragic if we were to sacrifice the
voice of our hearts at the altar of science. Moltique
realized I was forwarding a counterargument, albeit
one disguised as a meek question. He did not reply,
and that disturbs me. I want to believe that he is
sure of what he plans to do. I am surprised that
an experienced and esteemed scientist like him,
albeit one who is sensational and controversial, is
not more critical of his own ideas. I do not think

I should offer criticism, either. That is why I keep my thoughts to myself, all the while endeavouring to extract more basic information from Moltique regarding research into human beings and life.

The year is illegible, but going by its contents the entry dates from 1820.

I worked hard today. I went through the notes I had written for Moltique and saw that after our landmark discovery in May we had made slow but sure progress. When we spotted the first footprints, which had left depressions in the wet soil, we drifted too far east, but once we found new prints, locating the cave was easier. Going over my notes, I realized that following the discovery of the cave quite a lot of time passed before we first caught sight of the children. I wondered why. Did the creatures sense our presence and hide? Or had they perhaps left the cave in order to hunt and gather food? (We know the children eat meat, insects and parts of plants.) Maybe they are nomads and only reached the cave this spring. We have not clarified with what animals their habits link them.

So far, we have made do with observing the cave and its inhabitants through a telescope, because if we get too close the children retreat. From the observations I had written down for Moltique, I established that we had identified ten different children. I have noted their animal features: for example, Object No. 1, boy, tusks; Object No. 2, boy, ears like a cat's.

I arranged the notes so that our travelogue now forms one unified entity and our observations on the children another. I keep my personal diary well away from the papers Moltique leafs through for his work. I have also started writing these entries in Russian, a language Moltique does not know.

JULY, DATE ILLEGIBLE, IN THE YEAR 1820

Today I followed the small girl into the forest, where I saw her gather something and put it onto a large leaf. I told Moltique about my observation and he asked what the dominant female, as he calls Petite, was gathering. I said I did not see, but I suspect she was picking either fungi or insects, because after she left I went to investigate the site and did not find any bushes or shrubs bearing berries. Moltique said that the information confirmed that the inhabitants of the cave behaved much like some monkeys he had observed. I am troubled by the way he obstinately compares the children to monkeys without taking into account that there could be another explanation for their peculiar appearance. I do not know myself what it might be, but one would think that a famous researcher like Moltique would have another theory in reserve. I fear his ambition blinds him. I am also worried about the Church's reaction, once he has published his findings. Amid this wilderness, it is hard to remember the realities of the civilized world. Moltique is not concerned about the reaction of the Church – he's utterly unconcerned, in fact, I'd say.

JULY, DATE ILLEGIBLE, IN THE YEAR 1820

The inhabitant of the cave I call Petite has entered
my dreams. She looks at me entreatingly, asking
for something. I cannot make out her speech. Is it
speech? I woke up this morning covered in sweat,
my heart thumping, for there was something terrify-
ingly human in the eyes of the creature I saw in my
dream. I have tried to forget the carcass of the creature we felled in May, but it haunts my mind and
gets muddled with my thoughts of Petite. Moltique
cut up the boar-like creature we shot, preserving the
most interesting parts in glass jars in order to take
them to Paris later. This was no doubt right and
necessary for his work, but I am troubled by the fact
that the remaining parts of the carcass were fed to
the guides' dogs rather than being given a decent
burial in the forest, as was my proposal.

Some time ago, I had a dream in which my dog,
Noir, rose to his hind legs and begged me for help
but, frighteningly, I was unable to understand him,
or to assist. I had had to leave that loyal creature in
the care of my landlady's simple son upon quitting
Paris. Following that dream, my thoughts have every
now and then returned to my dog. I console myself
with the idea that, though Hugo is a simpleton who
at the age of twelve can still barely wipe his own
nose, he is also extremely gentle and good-hearted.
Also, it is useful for an idiot to be accompanied by a
dog as intelligent as Noir.

The same evening, as we sat by the fire, I told
Moltique about Noir. He asked with as straight a

face as he could muster if it was only a dog back
in Paris that I missed. Was there not a single girl
waiting for me? I have heard about his reputation
as a ladies' man and I felt abashed. But his guess
was correct: I have not felt a great need for romantic
relationships. My few relationships with the opposite sex have been short-lived and, to borrow a word
of my father's, fairly platonic (*amor platonicus*).
I think I am the same type of serious-minded man
as my father, who has always stood by my mother's
side, steady as a rock. I still hope and expect to
meet the woman of my life, though the chances are
not great, not as long as I am following Moltique on
his expeditions to uncharted territories. We have not
seen a representative of the opposite sex for a long
time. The women we last saw were prematurely
aged country folk in a small Prussian village – they
sold us potatoes.

Numerous entries from July and the beginning of August appear to have been lost.

One of our assistants got sick in July and failed to recover, despite the ministrations of our self-taught doctor, Pierre Rufin. On the contrary, he deteriorated rapidly. Moltique set off with a few of the other assistants to look for help, leaving me in charge of the camp. My task is to continue observing the cave and making basic notes. Moltique was not best pleased about having to interrupt his research, but he recognized his responsibility, which makes him a better human being than he is generally thought to be. The patient is indeed one of our most important men: Bruno Papart, our most skilled tracker and hunter. I am not sure if Moltique would have been as interested in the welfare of, say, Yves Grillet. Be that as it may, Moltique has already been away for nine days and I have tracked the movements of the cave's inhabitants faithfully. They have been on their guard, though, and I have only managed to see them on a few days, and even then just for a moment. I have begun to suspect that the cave has another entrance, or that sunlight can filter inside, so the children do not want or need to go out every day. While we have named the inhabitants children of shadows, I cannot conceive of a human being who would voluntarily sit in the dark.

I thought of dispatching one of the assistants to circle the cave and look for another entrance, but I am not sure which of them I can trust. I can still hear their coarse laughter when Moltique came out with his joke about a child hunt. I do not know if they are just excited by the idea of killing a living being, or by the fact that these animals look so much like humans.

It is unfortunate, but the men who have ended up on this journey are better off outside the reach of officialdom. I am not upset by this observation, for I think it is better decent men with families stay at home. The men acting as our assistants also have skills rarely acquired by more learned and/or respectable men. I am grateful for what I have learned from them, but they are no conversationalists. That is why I anticipate even Moltique's prickly company impatiently. To cap it all, I am painfully aware that the rest of our party has scant respect for me. They are deterred from disobedience only by the esteem they feel for the professor. I dare not think what would happen if Moltique did not, for one reason or another, return to the camp.

Agolasky has described some of the men in Moltique's party on a separate piece of paper. The notes are short verbal caricatures; one imagines upon reading them that Agolasky would have wanted to immortalize the rogues in pictures, too. They appear to have been written at the start of the journey, for his own amusement. We append them here in order to elucidate Agolasky's concern for his own safety.

JAVIER

He whose mouth is always hanging open. Wordlessly, he watches what others get up to, and it is never quite clear how much he understands. But when it comes to snapping the neck of a game bird or slitting open a deer's throat, he acts quickly, without hesitation. He cleans his bloodied hands by licking them and I have never seen a more blissful expression than Javier's when his tongue tastes blood.

PIERRE

A drunkard who never stops sweating. His bald pate is ringed with a reddish-brown, curly tonsure, which joins an untidy, straggly beard under his ears. Pierre is our doctor and claims that he learned his profession while travelling in the East. I don't believe half of his bragging, but he is adept at putting a dislocated arm back into place or digging a splinter out of infected flesh.

BRUNO

Bruno is a hunter. Sometimes it seems he hears and smells more acutely than the rest of us. When he goes to get food for the camp, he always takes Javier and his hound, which has no name; the medium-sized, sturdy, black-and-white animal answers to Dog. Among these repellent scoundrels, Bruno makes a favourable impression. There's something humane, even intelligent about him. I believe he is the son of a fisherman and hails from a village near Nantes. I do not know where Moltique picked him up.

YVES

Yves is a crook. He is capable of anything. He is not necessarily violent, but he is good at creating a bad atmosphere and stoking up dissension among the men. He has a bright, angelic face and large, chocolate-brown eyes edged with long eyelashes. You might think that a man so beautiful would be incapable of evil, but I say that Yves is rotten through and through.

FIST

If I could draw, I would begin a depiction of Fist from his chest. I would draw it large and convex like a barrel. His shoulders are broad, his arms muscular and his hands big and red. His thick neck leads to a small, bald head with two bright blue, cruelly gleaming eyes. If you see Fist – real name

Gabriel – turn his gaze on you, leave, for it's a bad sign. He wants either to complain about something or to slap you in the face. Longer contact would cost you your life, for Fist has as much strength as a small village. He is rumoured to have killed his faithless old lady and her lover, the former with one of his fists and the latter with the other. I do not want to know any more about him.

PAUL

Paul is slight but has a big mouth. He is a harmless and, in his own way, amusing rogue who always agrees with the previous speaker. He should not be among these criminals, for he is quick to learn. He is said to be the orphan son of a poor man, and he made a living by singing in the street and performing short one-man plays before Moltique recruited him for our expedition.

SIMON

A sex-mad young man who would be better off somewhere else. All Simon talks about is It and doing It. Ah, I know no one more boring than him.

BALLS

Jean Roux – or Balls – is hung with impressive male equipment which no one with eyes in their head can fail to notice. Even in this company, his need to lift and adjust his testicles is conspicuous. Whatever his secret is, it's certainly not his gigantic member.

I should not laugh at him, for the poor man seems embarrassed by all the attention...

COOK

At least this messy and indifferent lazybones has not yet managed to kill us! Sometimes the food is good, even excellent, but you do not want to see how carelessly it is prepared. I have heard that Cook joined us because he was being hounded by creditors. He is said to have lived in some style on his ill-gotten gains until he had to flee. Some say that once our expedition is over he will return to Paris to find his cache, which will enable him to continue his comfortable life. I personally think that he is merely trying to make the others envious.

The contents would indicate the following undated entries were made in August.

It has rained for several days. Our camp has become a sea of mud, the rocks by our toilet are perilously slippery and the moss in the surrounding forest has become a bog. The walls of our tents hang sodden and are beginning to leak; we cannot use our log cabin because the new dormitory wings are not complete. It has been warm and dry from May to August and we have not been in any hurry with the cabin. The unexpected discovery of the cave dwellers delayed the completion of the camp, but we have to finish the cabin as soon as the rains cease. In this region, winter is snowy and cold.

Despite my permanently damp hands and swollen fingers, I try to keep up with the diary, to pass the time. I do not want to join our assistants, to listen to them spouting obscenities about both women and men, all the while picking their noses and nails and digging into their crotches. I wish I could draw, so as to immortalize this unkempt, slack group of men. No words can describe them. I have tried to keep the fellows busy by inventing tasks for them, but they come across as lazy and ineffectual. Fortunately, a few of them carry on with their daily jobs in the usual way, despite the rain. I saw one of them carrying a willow grouse from the forest, so at least we shall get fresh meat for dinner. There has been no sign of Moltique and his party, and I cannot help wondering how long their journey will take. Because of the rain, I have not seen the cave dwellers, either, and I have a nagging fear they have gone. I cannot imagine Moltique's disappointment if this turns out to be the case. I am pretty sure he will hold me responsible.

Moltique's absence has given me the opportunity to sort out my thoughts. I realize my emotions have got the better of me and that I have failed to examine matters scientifically. So I decided that, as soon as the weather clears, I will try to obtain more information about the occupants of the cave in order to understand to what extent they are animals and to what extent humans. Then I shall find it easier to respond to Moltique's theory and criticize it constructively, if need be. So far, we have observed the creatures from a distance, and I wonder how we can get closer. They are timid and seem capable of avoiding us, though we have tried to stay hidden and to approach them from downwind. I wonder, could I inure them to my presence by positioning myself in the same spot every day in full view of them? I assume that, if I do not act threateningly but merely sit still, they will at some stage become curious and try to approach me. Perhaps I should take something edible to offer them.

I am excited by my plan and wait impatiently for the weather to clear up. I sincerely hope the occupants of the cave have not left their dwelling place and are still there.

UNDATED

I was woken from my nap by a disturbance at the
camp. Rushing towards the fire, I saw some of the
men trying to catch one of our dogs, which was
dragging something light and furry. When the men
finally managed to prise the corpse off the dog, it
was badly soiled. I joined the group, at first thinking
that the dog had caught a large hare in the forest,
but something about the mouth of the muddy creature made my blood freeze. I asked the men to bring
the corpse out of the rain. With Pierre Rufin, our
quack, I carried it into the tent Moltique uses as his
study and placed it on the folding table. I forbade
the others from coming in, to allow myself time to
think about what Moltique would like me to do
with the corpse. I went to get my writing equipment
and noted down everything I had seen as precisely
as I could, also drawing a picture of the specimen
to the best of my ability. Yet again, I cursed the
inadequate means of depiction available to me, for
I still cannot say what the creature on the examination table was. I would definitely not classify it as a
monkey. It was sixty-five centimetres long, around
five kilos in weight and completely covered in blond
or light grey fur – I could not be sure of the colour
because the corpse was filthy, having been dragged
on the ground by the dog. It had four paws, one
torn off by the predator, long ears and a stubby
tail. But the facial features of the creature… At this
point, I have to take a deep breath, realizing I still
feel sick. In the skull, where you would expect to see

a normal hare's nose, eyes and large front teeth, I saw a human child's blue eyes, snub nose and small toothless mouth. I made sure of the latter aspect with Rufin's help; he pushed his fingers into the corpse's mouth and opened it. We both thought the gums, the palate and the tongue were by and large those of a human being. I had to leave the tent and go outside to vomit. When I returned, I found Rufin cursing coarsely, perspiration trickling down his bloated, reddening face. I did not like what I was hearing. It sounded as if he was planning to summon a group of men to the cave there and then in order to slaughter all the occupants. I gave him a stiff drink from Moltique's reserves and invoked the professor's authority. In this way, I got Rufin to cut up the corpse and preserve the parts in jars for Moltique's research. I myself went to find out who had killed the creature, but I did not get anyone to confess. I was led to believe that the dog found the dead body in the forest. I hope that really is the case, though I still wonder about the actual cause of death.

In the evening, I went to great pains to assure the men that the corpse belonged to a normal, albeit malformed hare. I saw from Rufin's reticent expression that he would have liked to say a word or two but was held back by the respect he felt for Moltique. I thought I had gained a little bit of time. I still pray silently for Moltique's imminent return.

I find I am afraid, but cannot say of what, precisely. The discovery of the baby-faced hare has shaken my conviction that the occupants of the cave possess a human quality over and above individual physical traits. Both of the carcasses that have been chopped up at the camp resemble animals more than human beings – that, at least, I can swear to. It gives me some peace of mind.

AUGUST 27TH IN THE YEAR 1820

I have been observing the cave for a number of days now. The first morning, I went closer to it than ever before and sat down on the ground to wait. I had with me a blanket, a piece of dry bread and some water, though I wondered if I would dare make any movement, even to have a drink. It would be better not to have to stand up to empty my bladder; I did not want to alert the cave dwellers to my presence through any sort of activity.

For several days, I saw no signs of life in the cave and I began to suspect that the occupants had left. Then, one day, I saw some movement inside the cave mouth, in the dark. I was quite certain of that, though for the rest of the day I saw no one and nothing. I returned to my spot the following day and the day after that. Finally, today, the first nosy creature slipped cautiously outside. I observed excitedly the small furry creature whose body shape closely resembled, to my mind, a human being – but it was moving on all fours and sniffing the air, face upturned. It did not come any closer and, after a short while, the boy/male (I prefer the word 'boy') whose back was covered in thick fur came to take it (him/her?) inside again. The gesture showed caring.

It made me think of my eldest cousin, Natalia.
When we were children, she was the only one of the
brood of cousins to wait for me as I, the youngest,
tearfully trotted after the others in the forests surrounding our summer villa, all scratched knees and
hands. Natalia would help me over tree trunks and
brooks, through thickets and thorny shrubs. She
also looked after me later, when I was bigger, wilder
and more capable. I realized that I had never appre-
ciated her care. If I could, I would go and visit her
immediately upon returning home, taking her some
chocolate – she'd have loved that. But Natalia died
years ago, of pneumonia, and I can only reminisce
about her long-suffering gentleness towards me.

I recalled the way the tall boy had lifted up the
small creature and carried it back to safety. Caring
for smaller, weaker beings is a human quality, as
I wrote in my notes. True enough, many animals
protect their young, but are there examples of the
young looking after each other? Once again, I realize how limited my knowledge is. It also occurs to
me that we have not seen any adult examples of
the species. There are many things I've not given a
single thought to because I've been assuming that
Moltique takes every possible angle into considera-
tion. But he does not deem it necessary to tell me
everything, which is naturally a little awkward,
because it is my task to keep a record of events. I
assume that he will dictate his report to me when he
is certain of his theory. Until now, he has wanted to
write the notes relating to the intermediate stages of
his research himself. I think that he somehow fears

me interfering with his work and perhaps affecting its progress. I cannot say I blame him. My attempt at making the cave dwellers accustomed to my presence deviates completely from Moltique's instructions. I hope my disobedience will be forgiven when I present him with a great deal of new information on his return.

I have dispatched a couple of our assistants to look for the second mouth of the cave. One-day excursions have so far yielded no results; I think they will have to make a longer trip and stay overnight. I wonder how I can ensure that they obey my order not to enter the cave if another entrance is found. The geographical distance from the camp may render them reckless and cause them to forget their instructions. After all, that's what has happened to me following Moltique's departure.

The diary note below is largely illegible because the page
got wet and the ink spread.

– the food I left has been taken away, but that
does not prove much. After all, hares and elks eat
branches put out for them without fear of hunters.
I worry that Petite has left the cave. Or should
I say the rest of the herd? Is there a connection
between the creatures concealing themselves and
Petite's absence? It makes you think –

– the men came back from their excursion – My
theory about another entrance to the cave has been
borne out.

An excellent September day. I had again taken bread
and water with me, and also my mother's hand
mirror. Following the disappearance of the bread,
grain and cured fish I had left by the cave, I wanted
to test how the cave dwellers reacted to other goods.
Annoying that there was nothing going spare in
the camp. My mother's hand mirror was a beloved
memento that I cherished, but I knew she would
understand the value of the sacrifice in the event of
its disappearing into the cave.
I came to the cave and took up my usual position
directly before the entrance, a place where I was

easy to spot. I sat there all day, not seeing or hearing anything apart from the natural environment. I practised drawing the flora close to my observation point, because the limitedness of my documentation methods grieves me more every day.

Eventually, when the autumn afternoon began to fade, I got up onto my stiff legs, placed my mother's mirror on a stone and left.

Now I am sitting here in my tent. I forced myself to eat a portion of hare, though I had trouble swallowing the meat after that recent episode. The food is swirling in my stomach and I feel restless. I can hardly wait till tomorrow. The whole camp is gripped by a tense atmosphere. The men are waiting for Moltique's return, because they want to know what to do in respect of the other cave mouth. I said the decision was Moltique's: before we hear from him, we do nothing. I had other plans for myself, though. I'm just waiting for a suitable opportunity to go on an overnight excursion by myself.

SEPTEMBER 7TH IN THE YEAR 1820

I left for the cave very early in the morning, almost running the four kilometres' distance. When I arrived at the cave, I saw a number of creatures hurry back in. To my joy, I also thought I saw Petite's small, upright figure among them.

The mirror was still on the stone where I had left it. For a moment, I felt bitterly disappointed, but then I saw that a beautiful leaf gilded by the autumn had been left on top. It could have floated there of its own accord, but a perfectly round, white stone placed upon it indicated otherwise. Was it a gift? A gift for me? From whom?

I sank to my knees and – I must confess – burst into tears. Not knowing gave rise to despair. In my mind's eye I saw both the two carcasses that we had cut up and Petite, busy with her tasks, and I did not know what to think of the occupants of the cave. Were they humans or animals? Or human animals? Animal humans? I pushed my fingers through my hair and damned both my own uncertainty and Moltique's certainty in respect of his ape theory. I decided to set out to look for the other mouth of the cave the following morning, without any further delay, though I didn't know how I would profit by it.

I took the leaf and the stone and replaced them with a small, dirty silk scarf I carried in my jacket pocket, weighting it down with a piece of wood.

SEPTEMBER 12TH IN THE YEAR 1820

The middle of the night and I am sitting in a brushwood hut I rigged up against a rock, by a burning fire. I dare not sleep. I have been away for two whole days now, looking for the other mouth of the cave – no luck today, either. I don't know if the men gave me poor guidance on purpose or out of sheer incompetence. I lied to them, saying I was going to finish the task Moltique gave me: spotting the grown-up members of the colony. This is partly true, because from the old observation point we have only managed to see the children of the cave (the young). Really I hope to gain new information about the occupants, perhaps even get closer to them. I am too agitated to carry on observing the cave in the old way. The mirror and silk scarf I left on the stone disappeared, but nothing was left in their place, to my great disappointment. It made me suspect that the leaf and the stone I found were there by chance, not a gift for me. I feel foolish and am again inclined towards Moltique's view of the cave dwellers as more animal in nature than human.

My departure was delayed by several days because, again, one of our assistants became ill. He eventually died, of rabies, Rufin is now certain. After some investigation, it emerged that the dog that had discovered the dead hare had previously bitten our man. When I asked about the dog, I was told it had died, too. Chagrined that I had not been kept informed of events, I gave the men a talking-to and, to my satisfaction, I detected a smidgen of respect in their postures and attitudes. I am Moltique's right hand; that helps.

I hope that in my absence the men don't associate the carcass I said was a hare with the cave and its occupants and so blame them for the dog and then our man contracting rabies. I am sure Rufin thinks as I do: Papart almost certainly fell victim to rabies. If that is the case, he must have died fairly soon after Moltique left camp with his party. What, then, is delaying their return? Apart from us, no one misses Bruno Papart; Moltique might just as well bury him in the forest and return to his work. I am growing rather anxious and note that Rufin, too, is thoughtful. He is not a pleasant man, but neither is he stupid.

Moltique and I have been roaming the sparsely populated regions of north-west Russia for a while already, living in the forest for the most part, but only now do I really understand that I am in the middle of an uninhabited wilderness. For a book-worm like me, this is a stunning experience, and I feel respect for the forest and its animals. I saw a bear beyond the clearing this morning. I had fallen asleep and my fire had gone out, which is why the beast had ventured so close. I watched it lifting its nose and sniffing the air just as the smallest inhabitants of the cave do, and again I thought Moltique was right, after all. Still, I ask myself, what small voice made me undertake this excursion to look for the other mouth of the cave, to wish for the impossible?

Writing in these conditions is difficult, so I shall finish.

SEPTEMBER 13TH IN THE YEAR 1820

Very early morning and still dusky. I was woken by the chill from the rock and decided to write to pass the time. I do not want to get moving yet – I'll wait for the wild animals to retire for their daytime rest. I slept for a few hours and dreamed again of my faithful dog, Noir. Longing fills my heart and I cannot help wondering that I do not miss any human being in the same way. I hope and trust that my parents are doing well without me. I have no close friends. In Paris, I was perhaps closest to Jean-Victor, who dreams of becoming a painter. That romantic fool never let me go to sleep at a decent hour, instead waxing lyrical on cheap wine. I have never heard anyone lavishing such praise on English landscapes. If I miss my dog, Jean-Victor seemed to miss those landscapes as another misses his beloved. No wonder – I have seen his landscape paintings and their beauty leaves you speechless. I wish, on this journey, that I had Jean-Victor's pictorial talents. Or that I had Jean-Victor with me to immortalize everything I have seen. These forests, pines, spruces, bears, foxes, capercaillies, Siberian jays – I should like to remember them all. I keep on writing, but I fear that when I return to Paris the words will have faded and their power vanished. And what if the mystery of the cave dwellers is never solved? Shall I believe afterwards that I have seen those two bizarre hybrids of man and beast, those sad figures whose humanity I want to believe in, without evidence? Why, I ask myself now? Why could I not be passionately interested in our research subjects even if they were animals? I do like Noir and I miss him. No, the reason lies in the fact that I have mistaken the cave dwellers for humans too many times. Some things, observations I have made, something in me seems to argue – against probability – that I have been dealing with humans. Am I, then, a romantic daydreamer like Jean-Victor, that devoted admirer of rolling cornfields? I have cursed Moltique's scientific hard-headedness, but in reality it is a blessing. What on earth would the two of us be doing in this wilderness if we were both emotional weaklings with a penchant for romanticism? Our assistants would have killed us both long ago.

I finish the morning's jottings with this gloomily self-ironic thought and start dismantling my camp. I look forward to the day's developments with excitement. I believe I am half a day away from the cave mouth discovered by our men. They had not seen any movement there, and it was my task to discover whether this entrance had any connection with the cave and its inhabitants.

SEPTEMBER 14TH IN THE YEAR 1820

I am exhausted and irritable. I think I found the other cave mouth today, right at the end of the day, but the site yielded nothing out of the ordinary. I do not want to return to the camp empty-handed, but I am worried about Moltique getting back before me. I need to find more information about the cave and I am hoping I shall be wiser after tomorrow.

An addendum: Night. I am trying to write, by firelight perforce – the circumstances do not make it easy. I can't sleep any more, because I woke up and could swear that a human, a child, was standing close to the fire staring at me. At the moment I cannot do anything, only wait to see if I shall find out who is interested in me – and why.

SEPTEMBER 16TH IN THE YEAR 1820

The small hill beyond which we have located the cave and its occupants is rocky and steep. Where the entrance to the cave on the other side is both wide and low, on this side of the incline it is very narrow, almost only a crack in the rock, and well hidden behind a spruce, just as our assistants said. I would not have spotted the crack were it not for the modest track of trampled-down moss that led to it, and the spruce in front with the broken-off branches.

I sat behind a rock nearby, hoping to see something or someone coming or going through the crack. I stuck to my observation point all day without seeing a great deal apart from a squirrel, which took an interest in me and approached me more and more fearlessly the longer I stayed put. In my boredom, I fed it far too many nuts from my diminishing provisions.

Now I am sitting by the fire in my modest camp, wondering what to do next. My excursion feels futile and I can only hope that I shall succeed in surprising my secret observer this coming night. I also wonder whether Moltique will dismiss me when he finds out I have left both the cave and its inhabitants unobserved and our assistants unsupervised. I miss my parents and the carefree years of my childhood as I have not done for a long time.

SEPTEMBER 17TH IN THE YEAR 1820

Today, I decided to pass through the crack. I had
to bend down and turn sideways to get in, and
ended up in a cavity that was too low for me to
stand upright in. I twisted and turned awkwardly
in my cramped space and felt the rock face with my
hands. Nothing. I had to fall onto my knees before I
found a passage close to the ground. To get into it,
I would have had to drop down onto my stomach. I
was too frightened to squeeze into the dark, narrow,
unfamiliar passage, and I wondered who else would
use such a difficult route. If the trampled path and
broken branches had not indicated otherwise, I
would have been prepared to believe that the crack I
had discovered was not, after all, the second mouth
to the cave. I returned dejectedly to my observation
point behind the rock, where the familiar squirrel
found me and stayed, optimistically, to wait for its
nut. I shooed it away crossly, fully aware that I was
venting my anger about the unsuccessful expedition
on a harmless, blameless creature.

I have come back to the fire to examine the map
of the area that we drew. The crack appears to
be located on the same side of the hill as the cave
mouth we have been observing so far. It therefore
seems likely that the crack and the cave are connected. Because the cave dwellers only appear at the
other entrance, I believe that the crack serves mainly
as a way in, rather than out. If my deduction is correct, I wonder why the path remains trampled.

SEPTEMBER 20TH IN THE YEAR 1820

I am greatly concerned that my excursion to the
other mouth of the cave has gone on too long. I
keep wondering whether Moltique has returned and
what he thinks of my absence from the camp. I hope
he will forgive me, nevertheless, if I can solve the
mystery of the figure observing me. The nightly visi-
tor has been cautious and stayed too far away for me
to imagine I could catch him or her (it?). However,
the creature is clearly curious, and I assume that one
night he or she will become reckless.

SEPTEMBER 21ST IN THE YEAR 1820

Petite is human! She speaks my native Russian,
albeit a little awkwardly, because her tongue resembles a parrot's in its thickness. I finally caught
her last night. I put the fire out, so it was darker,
and pretended I was asleep. When she crept close
enough, I got up and jumped at her. She was quick,
but not quick enough. She was small and light; I
was afraid I had hurt her, pinning her down like
that. At first, she let out a screech that did not
resemble any human sound. When I demanded
to know what she wanted from me – initially and
automatically in French, then only afterwards in
Russian – she started begging for mercy in my
beloved mother tongue. I let go, surprised, and
looked into her small face. I asked, 'What did you
say?' She replied, 'Have mercy, don't hurt me. I am
responsible for the children.'

Unfortunately, several pages of the diary appear to have gone missing. However, on the basis of surviving extracts, the following pages and letters sent by Professor Moltique from St Petersburg to the Académie des Sciences – which have been preserved in the academy's archives to this day – it is possible to infer that at the same time as Agolasky was making the discovery confirming his theory that the cave dwellers were human, Moltique had occasion to present his own ape-centred observations to French scientific circles. These thoughts – put forward over thirty years before Darwin's theory of evolution was developed – must have provoked enough condemnation for the recipient to feel obliged to hide them away, or else the academy did not want Moltique's observations to prompt discussion about the validity of the contemporary French natural scientist Jean-Baptiste Lamarck's early, controversial theories of evolution. Moltique did not learn of the fate of his letters, though as an experienced scientist he was no doubt aware of the competition, envy and – ironically enough – narrow-mindedness that are prevalent in scholarly circles. Presumably, Moltique still imagined that he would get reinforcements sent to the camp when he wrote to Paris, not guessing his discovery would remain a secret. The notes do not reveal Moltique's thoughts upon hearing of Agolasky's success in communicating with the children. Did he fear, like Agolasky, that members of the Church and sensation-seekers would invade the camp? And if he did, was he more worried about the children's fate or that of his theory of an intermediate species between man and beast? Did he fear for his position as a famous researcher?

Agolasky's time in the camp became torturous following Moltique's revelation; and he could not know, in 1820, that Moltique's letters would not reach the hands of the young reporter Oliver Alleg until late 1822 or early 1823 – with fateful consequences. As far as Jean-Baptiste Lamarck's theories of evolution were concerned, Alleg was an enthusiast.

APRIL 5TH IN THE YEAR 1821

Months have gone by since the horrific day when Moltique revealed that he had sent the letter to Paris. Ever since, I have been dreading the arrival of reporters and Church officials at the cave, although each new day fuels my hope that Moltique's letter failed to reach its destination.

The winter was tough both mentally and physically, because – as I have indicated – the severe frosts forced us to fight for our lives and scale back our research activities. I leafed through my diary today, noting the long, detailed description of Rufin's amputation of the frozen toes of two of our men. In winter, I pondered over what we would do with the crippled assistants, but I have come to see that anxiety over their own uselessness has made the men try their best. They clamber out of bed even before it is advisable. This morning I saw them carrying out their allocated tasks diligently – which increases my respect for these foul-mouthed scoundrels with whom I would not normally associate.

Today is a warm, sunny day in early spring and the thawed patches of ground at the outskirts of the forest have grown in size. Earlier, I sat on a sun-warmed stone holding a mug of hot tea, enjoying the iron smell of melting snow. I feel better in many ways. Not only have no outsiders appeared in our camp, but Moltique is talking to me again, which is a relief. He is also working with fresh enthusiasm, now I've got him interested in the cave dwellers and listening to my theories, which are supported by Anna's[*] tales:[†] the children were born to normal people all over Russia and their bodies displayed different variants at birth. Our observation that some children's animal features are more visible is accurate. Anna has discerned that the extent and the level of the animal features of the children's bodies (and minds?) affect the length of their lives. The more animal they are, the more quickly they reach the end of their lifespans and die. Anna does not know the reason for this, and why should she? She is merely a victim of this phenomenon, and as the

[*]   Anna is the cave dweller Agolasky earlier dubbed 'Petite'.
[†]   Since Agolasky's own diary has largely been destroyed, it is fortunate that his suspicions induced him to keep several notebooks and hide them in different places about the camp. So a separate set of records, *The Children of the Cave: Life Stories*, was preserved in its entirety and discovered in the archives of the Académie des Sciences while background research was being carried out during the editing of the diaries. No one had previously linked it to Moltique's letters regarding his ape theory and the diary was filed in the archive under the key word 'fairy tales'. It was thought that the stories were products of Agolasky's imagination and that he wrote them to while away the time, bored by the monotony of camp life – this despite Agolasky describing the children's measurements in relation to his own size; simple drawings show how tall each child is compared with Agolasky.

oldest child, in fact as a young adult – she calculates her age at nineteen years, not much younger than I – has taken responsibility for the other children of the cave.

Anna recollects having lived in the cave for five years, and she has seen children come there to live and die. There is a rumour among parents of variant children that there is such a cave where the children can be left. With one exception, the parents do not return to ask what has befallen their offspring. It is better this way, because among the populace the children's fates are heart-rendingly miserable. That goes even for those who have only been burdened by the faintest hints of animality: feathers on their sides, fur on their backs or, as in Anna's case, an animal tongue. A child born deformed arouses fear and shame and is hidden from people's eyes or, even worse, killed there and then. A comforting legend is in circulation among the children: a hero roams the world overcoming perilous situations with the help of his poisonous fangs and ability to fly. A snake's and a bird's – or bat's – features, in one child? The story probably has no basis in reality, because, going by Anna's and my own observations, the children possess only one animal feature each. And so my nightmare about a hybrid incorporating characteristics from several different animals remains just that, a nightmare. For the children, however, this versatile hero grants hope that they, too, could perform miraculous feats. The wretched truth is that they are condemned to live in shadows, hidden from people's eyes.

I have been thinking repeatedly about ways of getting help for these children; I am becoming more attached to them than is advisable. I try to hide my feelings from the professor, who approaches the children with scientific coolness, not mourning the dissected *research specimens*, as he insists on calling the deformed children. I believe he would be happy to do the same thing again. Though our approaches are totally different, I do respect his tireless quest for a theory that would explain the animal mutations.

I do not like the way Moltique has started to talk about the children as werewolves, though; he says the werewolf theory is as serious a contender as that of the evolution of humans from animals – for example, apes. *Lupi manari*, he said, and told me about both people who become wolves and wolves who resemble people. I protested: the children don't all look like wolves, nor do they behave like predators. He nodded knowingly and commented with a greatly satisfied air, 'Perhaps these children prove that werewolves are as real as the yeti. The word "wolf" gives the wrong impression, though. We are talking about human *animals*. I do recall hearing at some point about a man who changed into a hare.'

He informed me that there were two views of werewolves: according to one, some humans assume the form of a wolf in order to do harm to other humans; according to the other, such folk have been cursed and they change into wolves as a consequence. I knew that already, but my father had always assured me that werewolf stories were super-stitious nonsense. But Moltique shut me down, again pointing out that he of all people knew from experience that that which is incredible can prove to be true. He did concede that he did not think the children wanted to harm anyone, whereas all the stories he had heard about werewolves involved terrible killings, murders and torture committed with relish. The most likely theory was that some unknown curse had caused the animal mutations in the children.

As a learned man, Moltique should be able to identify the magician, and the reason behind the magic, before declaring magic the cause of the mutations. The possibility of a mutation is also excluded by several factors, at least in the case of the individuals we have studied: as far as we know, none of the children with animalistic properties changes completely into an animal, as in Ovid's *Metamorphoses*. I am annoyed that I cannot remember the details of the story, which my father read to me, among many others. I have realized that scientific work does not involve one orthodox line, nor are there just a few skills associated with particular branches – rather, everything is connected to everything else. I miss my father's wide-ranging knowledge of literature as badly as I do Jean-Victor's pictorial talents.

I understand Moltique's disappointment at being compelled to abandon his theories concerning the evolution of man. However, I respect him more as a man and an explorer because he is able to be humble in the face of the things he has seen and heard. As an ally, he is steadfast; as an enemy, frightening, even dangerous, as I have seen. I have used all my powers of persuasion to get to the point we are at now: Moltique talks to me these days, though he makes sure I know my place, by making me run more and more little errands for him. I tolerate all this because we still have much to do. I am also trying to forget the beating I got back in winter, though I still cannot face the men Moltique put up to the job. The scars on my back and my legs will remind me for the rest of my life of how an uneducated herd of men can crush a person who thinks too highly of himself. I am not surprised to discover that side to the prestigious professor of the Académie des Sciences, because I could sense it at our first meeting – that is why I was chosen for this role, I think. My ambition and lust for adventure make me more fearless than I imagined I was. Or perhaps I am merely more dim-witted than the average fellow.

CHILDREN OF THE CAVE

ANNA

Sex: female
Age: around 19
Animal trait: a parrot's tongue
Narrator: Anna
Recorder of the story: Iax Agolasky (me)

From her childhood, Anna remembers a small house at the edge of a forest. The house had two bedrooms, a low-ceilinged but comfortable living room, a dining room and a small, cosy kitchen. It was just the two of them: herself and a woman she called

Auntie. The woman smelt nice and always spoke in a gentle, croaking voice. Only later did Anna learn that Auntie was unable to raise her voice, to shout or give orders or hiss like an angry cat; she could only babble and burble softly, like a brook, or pigeons in a dovecote. In her company, Anna got used to a world without angry human voices and ugly words, and in that world she herself was a perfectly faultless little girl. Until the day she met a perfectly faultless little girl.

Anna had never strayed far from the house, because Auntie had set clear limits: she knew up to which point she could go on the narrow, sandy track, which ended with a carefully tended shrub and a gate. This was always shut, but one day a girl came along the sandy track right up to their veranda. She had dark hair, brown eyes and a white dress, and she looked quite as if she had invented summer. That's what Anna remembers thinking.

'Hello,' said the girl, and then she gave her name. Anna has forgotten it now; she only remembers the soft, white skin, the smile and the way the girl spoke. As if she were playing a pipe. The sound fell off her lips easily; it was full, clear and metallic – quite different from Anna's and Auntie's voices.

Then the girl asked about Anna's name and age. Anna was pleased, and she opened her mouth to divulge everything about herself, but before she had got to the end of her reply, she noticed the girl's expression: a mixture of disbelief and worry, with amusement bubbling gently underneath.

'Don't be silly,' said the girl.

Anna replied that she was not being silly.

The girl raised her eyebrows, which were narrow and very dark. 'Can't you speak?' she asked, pursing her cherry-red lips.

'I can,' Anna said, feeling hot tears prickling her eyes. Something was going horribly wrong between her and the pretty little girl, whom Anna badly wanted to have as a friend.

'You speak just like a baby,' the girl insisted.

'But I'm five already,' Anna protested.

'What?' the girl asked, bending closer. 'Have you got a potato in your mouth?'

Anna opened her mouth to show that there was no potato there; she had a tongue and teeth just like the girl, who had started to seem disagreeable. Anna was feeling annoyed that she had struck up a conversation with her.

'Oh!' The girl was horrified. She raised her hand to her face. 'Something's happened to your tongue.'

Anna was startled. 'What?'

'It got caught in a door.'

Anna didn't remember anything like that ever happening, but the girl seemed to know what she was talking about.

'That's why you can't speak properly,' the girl said.

She was convinced that was how things stood. To Anna, this information came as a shock. But she had no chance to argue because someone was calling the girl in an angry voice.

'I'm not supposed to come here,' the girl whispered, frightened. 'I've got to go.' She turned and began running.

Anna was about to go after her, but Auntie held her back. 'Come here, dear child,' she said, and Anna saw tears in her kind brown eyes.

Anna threw herself into Auntie's lap and burst into tears. Auntie tried to comfort her, saying she spoke perfectly well, but nothing she said could make Anna any less inconsolable, now that she had learned that she was different from the perfect little girl who lived beyond the hedge. Anna was not part of that world.

Agolasky added an illustration of Anna's tongue to her story; the shaky sketch shows that Anna's tongue closely resembled that of a parrot, being thick but soft.

NIKOLAI

Sex: male
Age: around 10–12
Animal trait: fur covering the body
Narrators: Nikolai and Anna
Recorder of the story: Iax Agolasky (me)

'We can't manage without Anna.' Those were Nikolai's first words when he sat down for the interview. I could understand him, but his speech was unclear; all the same, without his dense fur, he would be no different from an ordinary boy. He kept glancing around nervously and he watched me from under his brows, avoiding eye contact. He had a strong forehead, deep-set brown eyes and a nose with wide nostrils. I assured him that I would not harm Anna. He relaxed a little and began sucking a small bone. I asked him how he had got to the cave. He said he remembered a horse, and a man who would not address him and kept him in a cage, feeding him as if he were an animal and hitting him if he spoke.

'Do you remember your parents?' I asked.

A sad expression crossed his face. 'I remember Mother,' he whispered. 'I remember Mother running a high temperature. Mother was taken away and she never came back.'

'What happened then?' I asked, and my heart was gripped by fear.

And Nikolai told me. He spoke about an aunt and an uncle, who fetched him from home. Nikolai waited for them in the drawing room, wearing his best clothes. He bowed, shook hands and greeted them, trying to make as good an impression as possible. Auntie and Uncle marvelled at what a big, fine boy he was, and took Nikolai with them. They travelled for two whole days, spending the night in a rattling carriage and finally arriving at a large house surrounded by a splendid garden. It was dark and Nikolai was hurried to bed. He lay down in a bed with curtains and fell asleep straight away.

'In the morning, a vat was brought in and filled with a mixture of cold and boiling-hot water,' Nikolai said softly. I began to fear the worst. 'Auntie came into the room and told me to undress,'

Nikolai went on. His voice had become smaller and more blurred.

'Your auntie realized you were hairy all over,' I suggested, as gently as I was able to.

He nodded sadly, and I heard the depth of his heavy sigh.

'I had always thought I was a perfectly ordinary boy,' he said. 'Mother never said there was anything wrong with me.'

I waited, but he did not continue. Nikolai stood up abruptly and left me there alone.

I heard the end of the story – or was it the end? – from Anna.

'Nikolai had the same thing happen to him as I did,' Anna said.

Nikolai was locked in the outside cellar for several months before the dog-catcher came to fetch him. Then he was brought to the cave, left next to a spruce, and that is where Anna found him.

THE TWINS HUGH AND PUGH

Sex: male
Age: under 2
Animal traits: fur like a feral cat's on the back, long whiskers, tail-like fur on the lower back
Narrator: Anna
Recorder of the story: Iax Agolasky (me)

There are two delightful small boys among the cave dwellers. Anna, Nikolai and Katya call them Hugh and Pugh. They are small, light, very playful and very hairy on their backs and faces. Nobody knows their story because they were discovered in a potato crate outside the cave in the spring of the previous year. They were asleep in the box, curled against each other. They were thin and sickly and their fur was unkempt. Anna cleaned, fed and took care of them till they got stronger and began to grow. They do not speak but understand when spoken to. They like being stroked, scratched and cuddled. They push their noses against other children's necks, snuffling softly all the while. Anna and Nikolai wait eagerly to see if they will learn to speak. Each new day erodes their hope a little, but they have not yet given up.

I am sitting on the cave floor and Hugh and Pugh are busy around me. They have shiny white, sharp canines. They look happy and healthy, and I wonder what will happen to them if they are discovered. Would they receive more sympathy than in their lives up to now? I fear not.

ROBERTO THE LION KING

Sex: male
Age: if he is to be believed, at least 15 and maybe 20; but in reality 10–12
Animal traits: fur like a feral cat's on the back, long whiskers, tail-like fur on the lower back
Narrator: Roberto
Recorder of the story: Iax Agolasky (me)

Roberto the Lion King toured with Signor Battagia, who touted miracle cures. Roberto had lived and travelled with him for as long as he could remember, but Signor Battagia was not his father.

'I've had many women,' Signor Battagia would boast, 'dozens and dozens, dark and fair, from Naples to Florence, but children – no. I've always quit before a woman has started dreaming about a family, a field and a house in the middle of an orchard. These things I cannot offer. I have only my cart, my medicines, my sleights of hand and Roberto. Come and have a look at Roberto the Lion King. He speaks Italian, Russian, Arabic and, of course, the language of lions! Is he human? Is he an animal? Who knows? He's marvellous! Throw coins, bread or fruit into the hat, or leave a bottle of wine by the cart. You can pay with anything for this peculiar child, who'll never grow up!'

Roberto seemed to remember Signor Battagia's speech word for word; he puffed up his chest, grew taller than his real height, lowered his voice and slapped his thighs. I kept on writing, enchanted and amazed, though I do not know whether to believe half of what he says he saw and experienced.

Roberto was happy with Signor Battagia. Sometimes they ate well, sometimes badly; at times they were treated like welcome guests, at other times they fled for their lives.

'I've got to be at least fifteen, maybe twenty,' Roberto assured me. I did not say anything, though I could see his body was thin and small, like that of a child. 'Signor Battagia let me drink wine, smoke a pipe, kiss a girl and stay up till morning playing the mouth organ. Rosa said only grown men live like that.'

And when asked who Rosa was, Roberto waxed lyrical: 'Ah, Rosa! She's Signor Battagia's great love. She isn't a beauty but she has lovely round arms, soft shoulders, plump lips and she smells nice. How does she smell? Like a sandwich. She travels with us, cooks us porridge and macaroni, fries sausages and sometimes steals chickens.'

I do not have the heart to ask what happened to them and where they are now, Signor Battagia and Rosa. Roberto looks happy when he shows me how he picked pockets for coins; how he and Rosa ran, fresh loaves stolen from a baker under their arms; how he roared in his cage, waving his hands as if they were big paws; and when he demonstrates how Signor Battagia healed ague-sufferers and the blind, and turned unfaithful wives into goats.

'Roberto, are you happy?'

'I'll stay here until Signor Battagia comes and gets me,' Roberto answered me. 'Nikolai's a good fellow. The others are a bit odd, but Katya sees in the dark, so I'm sure Signor Battagia can use her one way or another – I'll take her with me.'

KATYA

Sex: female
Age: 12
Animal trait: sees in the dark
Narrator: Katya
Recorder of the story: Iax Agolasky (me)

Katya can see in the dark. She announces this in the
same way someone else might say they can read.
Apart from seeing everything, she also has a superior
sense of smell and can remember her whole life from
the moment she was born, surprising listeners with
her tale of how she felt upon arriving into the damp
heat of the sauna; being lifted up, washed and swad-
dled; the taste of the first mouthful of warm, sweet
mother's milk. She knows her date of birth: 2nd
July 1808. She is the daughter of the Kalatozovs; her
father's name is Mihail, her mother's, Anja. Father
is a teacher and the family live in a village close to
the Finnish border. Anja is Finnish. Katya says all
this in a soft, fragile voice. Appearing matter-of-fact
and sharp, she explains that she sees her parents
now and then. Disguised as pedlars, they come to
see how she is, bringing utensils. Katya cannot go to
her home village, for people there are afraid of her:
the women mumble prayers as she approaches and
the men try to work out ways of getting rid of her.
At the age of nine, Katya was stuck in a sinkhole for
a week, forced to live on earthworms and rainwater.
She would undoubtedly have died had her parents
not found her. Then Anja, or Anjuska, as her family
called her, heard about the so-called dragon children, and a cave where they could live in safety, and
she started making arrangements. She taught Katya
survival skills, hunting and fishing, and she pointed
out edible plants and plants with medicinal properties. She forced Katya to do exercises, run, carry
heavy objects, break birds' necks and make a fire by
striking two stones together. Katya never asked how

come her mother knew so much and was so capable. And when Mother decided Katya was ready, the girl vanished from the village. Then, three days after the disappearance, Katya's scarf was found in the river. No villagers came to extend their condolences to Anja and Mihail. They were pleased about the departure of the strange little girl who told weird stories and whose eyes glinted green in the dark. Anja and Mihail did not have to pretend they were heartbroken; they were genuinely frightened for their child, because that first winter was severe, there was a great deal of snow and they couldn't get to the cave to see how she was. They did not know if Katya and the other children were even alive. When spring finally arrived, they appeared at the cave mouth, bringing sweets, clothes, food and candles for their daughter. They were horrified by how animal-like she looked.

'I've been following you.' These are Katya's first words to me when Anna brings me into the cave. She adds, 'At night. You haven't noticed. You live with those men over there. You shot Buutje and cut him up. You put him in jars. Where are you taking Buutje?'

I look at the girl whose presence I have sensed. She appears to be a perfectly ordinary girl, although her eyes are slightly slanted. She has blonde curls, a small face and a pendant that indicates that some-body somewhere still cares about her.

'It's my mother's,' Katya says, lifting her hand to her neck. 'It belonged to my grandma, whom I never saw. She was Finnish.'

She asked where we were taking Buutje. I felt that old familiar terror. Where are we taking Buutje? Where will these children end up?

BUUTJE

Sex: not known
Age: not known
Other info: see notes concerning research specimen 1/1820
Animal trait: resembles a wild boar
Narrator: Katya
Recorder of the story: Iax Agolasky (me)

'Buutje would have been a fully-fledged wild boar had he not walked on two legs. He couldn't speak, sing or play games, but he loved to curl up between the others, press his snout against something and fall asleep while someone was scratching him. I loved Buutje. Buutje followed me around wherever I went,' Katya said evenly, without a trace of bitterness, sorrow or hatred. 'When I moved into the cave, Buutje lay down next to me the very first night.

'You were there,' she went on. 'You were there and you saw Buutje being shot. You recorded and described everything after Buutje's death.'

I nodded.

'Buutje wouldn't have lived long in any case,' Katya said. They all knew it.

The pile of notes that comprise *The Children of the Cave: Life Stories* is thick. Some of the stories are so grim we will not publish them here. At the same time as compiling these accounts, Agolasky was making notes daily in the camp. From the extracts that have survived, we can conclude that the occupants of the camp were suffering from exhaustion. Moltique had also forbidden the shooting of the cave dwellers, so we can imagine that the men, bent on excitement and adventure, were frustrated.

APRIL 6TH IN THE YEAR 1821

    – I do not like their talk. I hear snatches of talk that tell me they are ready and willing to harm the children, and are just waiting for a sign –

APRIL 7TH IN THE YEAR 1821

I surprised one of them, the giant known as Fist, in the act of stalking Hugh, one of the twins; he was crouching behind the bushes, boulder in hand. Hugh did not appear to sense his stalker's proximity and I wondered, momentarily worried, if my presence had accustomed the children to strangers and made them forget the caution that was necessary for survival.

    I cleared my throat and Fist turned, dropping the stone casually behind his back. I did not reveal that I had seen what he was up to. Instead, I said Moltique had asked me to come to the cave to check that everything was in order. I stressed Moltique's name and the words 'in order'. Fist swore and spat. I did not avoid eye contact, though I still remember how he enjoyed getting the chance to beat me with that thick branch back in winter, at the specific request of Moltique.

Then he left, but as he was passing he whispered something that made my hair stand on end –

APRIL 10TH IN THE YEAR 1821

Moltique seems irritated; I assume this is because he has not yet discovered a theory for the metamorphosis of the children of the cave, famous though he is for his swift conclusions and for the daring manoeuvres he has performed in support of his theories. His lack of friends in the Parisian scientific world is compensated for by his large number of admirers, this state of affairs being justifiable.

He may also be bothered by the fact that he has not managed to get close to the children but has to be content with my observations and unsatisfactory notes. He is doing everything to prevent me from seeing how my position... what? Arouses envy in him? Scientific jealousy? And perhaps something else? It is as if he is annoyed by the fact that just as I was experiencing my breakthrough in finding the cave entrance, he was wasting time on Bruno Papart, whose fate was sealed from the start.

I continue to suspect that Moltique has his own plans, which he is not sharing with me. Sometimes I wonder if he is really as interested in

metamorphoses and the magic that causes them as
he claims, or if he is misleading me on purpose. My
father taught me that man is fundamentally good.
Would that then mean that Moltique, being a man,
is also good? I try to remember my father's teach-
ings, but it is hard, here in the middle of the forest;
my thoughts disintegrate, like a reflection on water,
and I cannot keep up with them. I wish I could talk
about all this with my father!

UNDATED

I am confused. Anna makes me confused. She and
her... But no. It is best I do not say it aloud, or write
it, or think it. I will, however, note down this: her
eyes are green. More precisely: forest green, almost
brown, and a golden-yellow circle surrounds the
pupil. Her hair is dark brown, like a pine trunk;
reddish and yellow hairs are interspersed among the
darker ones. This has now been recorded. I go to
sleep, shivering with cold.

APRIL 15TH IN THE YEAR 1821

I had a strange dream last night. Everything I
watched turned into pictures, even sharper than
any drawn by Jean-Victor. Odd, because I have
never seen anything more lifelike or detailed than
Jean-Victor's drawings of Parisian streets and cafés,
dancing girls and old men napping on park benches.
When he occasionally borrowed my small room
to draw scantily clad women, I fled, embarrassed,

and found it hard to look at the sketches my friend proudly showed me – they were so lifelike. I never tired of marvelling at the way my friend could depict the smoothness of skin, the wild movement of hair, the flutter of thick eyelashes – and this using charcoal alone.

But in my dream, I had no charcoal or brush, just my eyes. I met each child of the cave separately. I looked at them long and hard in order that I would remember every detail of their singular appearance: fur descending beautifully from the cheeks towards the neck, curved whiskers, a black tip of a nose, a furry or feathery covering on shoulders or back. Then I blinked and everything I had seen transferred itself onto paper. It was magic, sleight of hand, delirium, dream. Could it be possible? I would have liked to ask Roberto the Lion King if Signor Battagia had performed such tricks. But no, how could that be?

To get rid of my strange thoughts I went for a walk. I inhaled the powerful smells of the thawing ground and admired the merry babbling of a brook emerging from under crumbling ice. It rained con-tinuously. (And still it rains, as I write this. At this rate, the last vestiges of the snow will rapidly thaw.)

When I got back, I noted how wretched our camp looks. The tents sag, waterlogged, no longer keeping out the rain. But as the days get longer, the conditions become more tolerable. I shudder to recall the long, harsh days of winter, when the morning darkness became evening darkness without a properly light period in between, just twilight at best. Writing these notes has offered me an unexpected lifeline.

APRIL 25TH IN THE YEAR 1821

– I pondered over Anna's responsibility for the children – how does she possess the strength – has she – She does not utter a single word of complaint about the fate faced by her and the others.

There is a separate piece of paper between the notes. The text it bears is not in Agolasky's handwriting. It was probably written by Anna, because the script is shaky and the unpractised hand has caused the ink to spread.

To dear Julia,

This is dedicated to my sister Julia. Not my real sister, but the one I shared my life with here. The one who spoke like my aunt and I. The one who croaked more than I ever did. Whose nose was made of a hard, bone-like stuff, whose eyes were black and round and whose cheeks were covered with short, fine down. And who was so big-hearted and wise, who comforted me and listened to me. She had one dream: to fly away from this place, which she called a cage. 'Where would you go?' I asked. And she said she would fly into the sky, higher and higher. And then she would be filled with emptiness and lightness, and nothing on earth would mean anything any more. She would be happy. That is why I did not grieve when she finally flew away. I knew she would be happier wherever she had gone.

APRIL 29TH IN THE YEAR 1821

I have been thinking about how I might help the children of the cave. Who would be interested in these life stories? Would anyone? Would they be treated as freaks, or works of the Devil, or subjected to scientific research? I feel inadequate, I, an insignificant assistant to a great explorer!

When I raised the issue with Moltique he lanced me with his mocking expression. He said there was no helping the children. At the same time, he revealed his new theory about the metamorphosis. He had studied the children's backgrounds in the light of what I had told him about them and had come to the conclusion that not a single one of them came from a normal, healthy family. I tried to protest, but he silenced me. 'Metamorphosis is nature's attempt to either finish off non-viable, imbecile families or change them into animals.' I asked why the phenomenon was present only in Russia and he laughed out loud. 'You're in Russia, idiot! Go to China, look diligently enough, and you will find a similar cave. Go to Italy, seek and you will find. Go –'

I raised my hand. I had understood. But then, after a while, I asked, 'What about France?' Moltique looked disgruntled. 'France,' he said thoughtfully. 'Our country is civilized, but... Who knows, maybe there's a similar cave there, too.'

He urged me to forget my dreams of rescue. I might as well plan to rescue the fish the men caught for our meals.

APRIL 30TH IN THE YEAR 1821

I asked Anna what she dreams of. She looked at
me tenderly and answered that she wished to be an
ordinary girl. And that she would have liked to say
goodbye to her aunt.

MAY — IN THE YEAR 1821

May – at last! I suddenly remember a day in Paris,
and what the air smelt like by the Seine, and how
wonderfully green the trees were. I was in love. No,
that is too big a word. I was infatuated, I was mad,
marvellously crazy, about a girl who sold fabric in
a small shop in the Marais. In the end, I was bold
enough to ask her out, and I took her for a picnic
in the park. We chatted for hours on end – about
what, I don't remember, but I do remember the
scent of her breath and the sound of her laughter,
which told me that she did not laugh often. Adèle,
that was her name. It was not love, for the sentiment
vanished when she moved away from Paris and I no
longer saw her. I went to visit her once. We went
to a park, as before; we laughed and chatted, but
something had changed. When we parted, I knew
I would not come again. Adèle seemed to know
it, too, but she did not appear any unhappier than
before. I never got to know her well; I did not learn
her secret.

   – Moltique asked me to take notes while he
thought aloud. He opened and closed his theory
of metamorphosis from its different angles, as if

folding a piece of paper. I wanted to say that we did not know enough about the children's families to draw conclusions about their imbecility, but I knew to remain silent. To tell the truth, I was impressed by the certainty with which the scientist I admired pursued the theory he desired. I could not help wondering what the truth was about the yeti and his other achievements.

– mad.

MAY 8TH IN THE YEAR 1821

– Moltique frightens me. I did not feel terror like this even when he ordered the men to take me into the forest to be flogged. I knew he needed me, his right hand. He leafs through his papers with a dissatisfied air, accusing me of inefficiency –

MAY 9TH IN THE YEAR 1821

I was on my way to empty my bladder when I heard a few men discussing the cave and its occupants. Fist was the most vociferous, but the others also had their say. They appeared to detest those animal-like humans. I heard Fist say that he did not believe the children could speak, that he thought I had invented the whole thing. And then he accused me of something that I cannot repeat even here. The thought uppermost in my mind was that Anna did not deserve such treatment. When I tried to continue on my way without making a sound, a branch snapped under my foot. I barely had time to hide behind a big rock before Fist emerged from beyond the tents to see where the noise had come from.

MAY 15TH IN THE YEAR 1821

Anna asked if they were in danger. I lied and said they had nothing to worry about.

MAY 16TH IN THE YEAR 1821

We have used up the liquor we brought with us from France and Moltique has moved on to spirits we have made ourselves. It is the rule rather than the exception that, come evening, he is in an advanced state of inebriation. Drunkenness makes him both more open and more unpleasant. He loves embarrassing me by analysing me. What a wretch I am in his eyes!

Home-made liquor is also distributed to the men more generously than the drink we brought from France, so the men are more often drunk these days as well. I do not really like –

Notes are missing from parts of May and June. The next set leads us to believe that in May the rebels among Moltique's men attacked some of the children, killing them cruelly. Either Agolasky was too shaken to write about the incident or time has destroyed the records.

JUNE 9TH IN THE YEAR 1821

Anna agreed to speak to me today. She did not say much and would not look me in the eye; I cannot blame her, given what has happened. I am not worthy of her trust. Still, she has recovered more quickly than I feared, but then she is obviously used to worse things than I.

On my way back from the cave to the camp, I made a detour to the children's graves. I was the only one who demanded that the children should be buried and the graves marked with their names. Even Anna did not support the idea. 'Why? Who misses them?' she asked flatly. I did not see her shed a single tear as we carried the bodies into the forest. She left me to bury the children alone in the holes and cover the bodies with earth.

I sat by the graves today, looking at the roughly carved names in the pieces of wood I had put up as gravestones: Petia, Miska, Sonja, Pekka. We did not mark the graves of the men who killed them. They could become soil, moss, trees and shrubs, and their memory could fade like the memory of plants and animals before and after them. Moltique agreed with me, though his anger sprang from different motives. 'You are wasting research material,' he thundered, but I could only stare at the blood on their stupidly grinning faces. I did not even hear Moltique sentencing them to death. And I did not hear them shouting in fear – or swearing – or being silenced by death. I was absent from this world until the next day, when I was woken up by Pierre Rufin dripping liquor down my throat.

Why do I write this, again? To help. How? To clarify my thoughts? I cannot think clearly. My world has shrunk to this corner of this Russian forest, home of the cave and the children.

JUNE 11TH IN THE YEAR 1821

Today, outside the cave, I saw Maksim and Boris. They were crouching, gathering leaves and grubs. They look almost like ordinary boys, though both have unusually large ears. I am not sure which animal's these resemble, but I have decided that one's are like a hare's, the other's like a mouse's. They took fright when they heard me approaching and fled quickly into the depths of the cave. The cave is labyrinthine and its walls have dark cavities where a small person can curl up and hide. I called the boys, but they did not reappear. It was quiet in the cave otherwise and no one turned up while I was there. I am sad I have lost the children's trust because of the men's cruelty. They are more than research subjects to me and the grief goes deeper that I believed possible. In my tent, I took out my notes about Maksim and Boris, surprised at how recently I had drawn them up.

MAKSIM

Sex: male
Age: around 7
Animal trait: hare-like ears
Narrator: Maksim
Recorder of the story: Iax Agolasky (me)

'I remember both of my parents well, because I've only been in the cave for a few winters. We had a small cottage in the middle of a forest, far from the nearest village. It was just us, on our own, and we had few visitors. We had a cow, a pig and a hen, and Father hunted animals for food, but only birds, no hares – not since he skinned a hare and I sat and cried by the carcass for a whole day, evening and night. My parents ate meat and eggs; I never did. That was the only thing about me that caused them to wonder. But because I grew well and was strong and healthy, they let things be. Because of my ears, Mother told me to pull on a cap if anyone came to our cottage.

One day, when they were busy doing jobs, a strange man came by. He had bizarre objects in his cart. He went inside and I hid behind the cart, because my parents had brought me up to be wary of strangers. The man was in our house for a long time, so I got a good look at the things he had with him. I identified the paws of various animals, horse hair, a cockerel's neck and a bag of feathers. Of the different things preserved in liquid, I could pick out a mouse embryo, a snake and eyeballs of various sizes, but there were also many items I did not recognize. The smell was unpleasant. I saw the man come out, peering about searchingly. For some reason, I was sure he was looking for me. When he set out towards his cart, I ran off as fast as my legs could carry me, but he had spotted me. I heard him coaxing me to come to him. But he didn't run after me, so I fled into the forest and hid there. I stayed there for several days, until one day I saw my father out on a hunting trip. He burst into tears upon seeing me, because he and Mother had thought the stranger had taken me: the man had come the next day to ask Mother and Father where their son was. My parents had lied and said they were childless.

I went home with Father. Mother bathed me and stuffed me with fresh bread and kept cuddling me. Finally, we all went to bed. We had been asleep a good while when we heard noises at the front door; someone was trying to open the latch. Father pushed me out through the waste hatch and I started running back into the forest. This time I heard the man setting off in pursuit of me. He was faster than I had thought and I became fearful that he would catch me, but then I heard him fall and I managed to slip into the darkness of the forest.

I did not dare go home this time. I lived in the woods for a few weeks, where Father brought me food and clothes. Then one day he came and said that he had heard of this place, a cave, where children who are different can live in peace. And so he brought me to the edge of the forest and took his leave. Neither of us cried then. I only cried when

I found the crack in the rock and knew I'd vanish from my parents' world for good.'

I asked Maksim if he knew who the stranger was. He shook his head.

'But I'm sure he would have liked to kill me and chop me up, to cure some of the pieces and preserve others in jars. Just as you do in your camp.'

I thought of the man Maksim had told me about and pondered over the things that were permissible in the name of science or greed. I also wondered if Moltique would recognize the man if I gave him a description.

BORIS

Sex: male
Age:13
Animal trait: mouse-like ears, unusually small, pink hands
Narrator: Boris
Recorder of the story: Iax Agolasky (me)

A man with a cart arrived at Boris's village, too. The cart had a canopy bearing the legend 'Popov Cures'. The man was thin with rotten teeth. He smelt bad, as well, but his wagon attracted a lot of visitors. He sold potions and powders with incredible powers.

'The women bought stuff to rub on their husbands' equipment,' Boris said, chuckling. 'Then they'd say the magic words Dr Popov had given them, and the man would get a terrible itch and either lose his whole tool or finally produce a male child. But Popov had other concoctions, too, that would fell an ox-necked smith, killing him dead, or make a gabby woman dumb as a goose. One nasty master was paralysed from the neck down, so he couldn't beat anyone up any more. The servants fed him his own shit, saying it was fresh bread.'

Boris was bursting with merriment, recalling all the events that would begin to occur in the village upon Dr Popov's arrival. He was still laughing as he told how his own mother had bought magic lotion that was supposed to make Boris's ears fall off his head, his pink protruding ears with the fur behind them.

'The lotion stung and felt ever so hot. It brought out blisters on my earlobes and made my eyes water – but my ears stayed put, redder than ever, only swollen now, too. Mother was disappointed. She'd spent most of her meagre savings on a miracle cure that didn't work. So she dragged me along to Dr Popov. She bustled through the village whirling up a sandstorm, skirts flapping like sails in the wind. We reached Popov's wagon but the man was nowhere to be seen. Mother called out for him, furious. Then she slapped the back of my head and told me to look in the tent that had been set up close to the wagon and, if Popov was in there, show him my ears. I was annoyed by the whole thing. I'd rather have been out fishing with Sergei and the others, but I did as I was told. I went over to the tent, stuck my head in… and surprised Dr Popov in the arms of a certain Nina Maslova. I may have giggled, because Popov pulled himself off her and nearly fell onto the floor. Then I saw something very strange.

Nina Maslova had an udder! Just like a cow. The udder was at the level where a woman usually has hair, and with her parted lips and sleepy eyes she looked like a cow that had stepped out of her skirt. Oh, how I laughed. I didn't stop even when Mother pulled me out by the scruff of my neck and boxed my ears. They stung already but I couldn't get Popov and Maslova out of my mind.

'Not long after, Maslova vanished without a trace. Just like that. And you can be sure she was a woman you'd notice. That's what Mother said. No one knew where she had gone, not even her own mother! One day, not long after her disappearance, I saw Dr Popov over the road. I thought he was cross with me because I'd seen Maslova and him at it, and I stayed safely indoors so he wouldn't get it into his head to come and lecture me. But the man just stood, looking towards our house. I got nervous. I couldn't think what Popov might want from me, but even so I was afraid. He lit a cigarette, spat onto the street and bit his nails – but he never once stopped staring at our house. Finally, I saw Mother bustling home. She hurried over to Popov – to demand her money back, I guessed. She shook her fist, and Popov made lewd signs with his hands, which confused me, knowing his popularity among the village women as I did: if he wasn't being referred to as Dr Popov, then he was Saviour Popov. Well, the scrap ended with Mother gathering her skirts and marching home. That was that, for the time being.'

As the story progressed, Boris was less and less inclined to laughter.

'Just a few days later, as I was coming back from fishing, Popov leapt out onto the path in front of me. I just caught a glimpse of him beckoning to someone behind my back – after that, I remember nothing… Until the moment I woke up here. In this cave. I remember Anna bending over me, saying there was no need to be afraid, I was safe. He, the man and others, had intended to make magic potions out of me. They had already cut off my little fingers – look! – and removed skin from several places. Do you see the scars? Do you? I remember nothing about it!'

Not remembering seemed worse to Boris than the actual danger he had faced. Terror shone from his eyes, as a forest fire lights up the horizon.

'But somebody somewhere rescues us: me and Nina Maslova – and everyone who is like these children. Can you guess who it is? It's The Spider, the canniest and most artful of us all. He'll come and get us. He'll take us from this cave to a place where there are no ordinary humans, only extraordinary ones. It's dangerous to be different where everyone else is alike. Have you noticed?'

JUNE – IN THE YEAR 1821

Moltique has made me work for days on end. I had to record all the stories he knows that involve a metamorphosis or some kind of combination of animal and man. I have listened to him, reminisced myself, combined, deduced, written and written again. Moltique said, among other things, that the notes of Herodotus, the chronicler of ancient Greece, contain entries about werewolves. 'According to Herodotus, the Neuri become wolves once a year,' Moltique ranted. He went on, with the same pathos, 'What about centaurs? Nothing but fairy-tale creatures? Not so: centaurs have been considered crosses between man and horse. But are they? Or have simple-minded nations merely depicted their conquerors on horseback thus? In that case, Iax, even in that case, they are real. Do you not concur?' But before I had time even to draw breath, never mind reply, he took a sip from his glass and whispered, 'And mermaids, Nereids, those seductive sirens of the deep. I have encountered them in my life, too. I truly believe so, though they say that I had been under the surface for several minutes before I was hauled aboard to safety. Why wouldn't I believe in Nereids, for their genealogy is noble, and historical notes document it? Their father is the eldest son of sea and land, Nereus, and their mother, Doris, a guardian spirit. Their history goes further back than that of Moltique... or the Agolaskys... You look surprised. Did your father not teach you anything?'

I wish we had access to my father's library, but when I made the mistake of mentioning this senti-ment to Moltique, he asked mockingly if his learn-ing wasn't enough. He also found time to describe his library to me: the length and height of the walls, the number of shelves dedicated to each genre, how much money he puts aside annually to replenish his collection, and so on. I realized I should not have

mentioned the great French scientist and an impov-
erished Russian scholar in the same sentence. I was
struck by longing, thinking of my father's gentle
eyes and large nose, of the spectacles he would
always push up on top of his head before looking
for them all over the house, and his hands – the
middle finger of the right hand was decorated by a
permanent ink stain. Was my father ever anything
but endlessly patient and supportive in my regard?
And still, how I had wanted to get away from home!
I cannot remember why. I wondered how they – my
parents – were. Do they miss me, do they fear for
me, do they reminisce about me as I do about them?

Today, while Moltique took a nap, I left hurriedly
for the forest so that he would not immediately find
me upon waking. I cheered up when I saw Anna,
gathering dry branches. I called her name and
she turned, smiling, but on seeing me, her smile
vanished and her eyes became watchful. I could
no longer bear it and asked her if she considered
me guilty of the men's deed. She said she blamed
herself. She should never have let anyone into the
cave. I asked her why she had. She said that perhaps
she had wanted people to hear the children's stories,
though she knew in her heart that no one could help
them. I observed her melancholy profile and wished,
more than anything in the world, that I could do
something for her. The sun was behind her so that
the loose strands of her hair shone like a halo round
her head. She was not the monster or the freak of
the stories, unable to speak properly, but a lovely,
wise, good girl who should have been allowed to live

among others, carefree. Thinking this, I came to wonder what my parents would think of her. And then, as if someone had poured cold water over me, I recalled something strange: I was small, perhaps two, and I had slipped between my parents in their big, soft, four-poster bed. I had had a nightmare and sought safety from Mother by stroking her hairy arm. Hairy? No, that was the wrong word: the arm was covered by slippery, smooth fur. I froze at the memory; even Anna noticed it. She asked if everything was all right and I replied that I wasn't sure. Had my mother also lived in shadows? What did my father think of her? Did I carry the same trait – and would my children inherit it?

I left the forest with conflicting emotions. I managed to avoid Moltique and went to bed. But I did not sleep all night.

The poem below is undated, but in view of the previous note, we might conclude that it came into being after the June day described above. There are no other entries from June.

> *In the forest, a bird: head, eyes, feet, like me.*
> *We're alike, my brother. Don't you see?*
> *Spread your wings, come over here,*
> *you've flown from afar, to be near.*
> *But will you stay or will you go?*
> *Myself, I have no choice – ah, no.*

UNDATED

I have been rather down, so much so that Moltique ordered me to rest. Has the man a heart and emotions after all? It is hard to credit. Perhaps he just wants to retain his faithful scribe. Upon crawling out from my tent, I smelt as bad as an unwashed man possibly can. I had urinated on my trouser legs and felt ashamed. It was unbearably hot and sultry; the July heat was at its peak, which made the situation worse. I went to the brook to wash. In other circumstances, I might have enjoyed the crackling heat in the surrounding forest, the coolness of the brook, the warm undergrowth exuding its heady smell. Now I felt wretched: miserable and powerless. I could see no way of escaping my unbearable situation and no opportunity to help the children of the cave. I dread to think what Moltique's plans for them might be. He has not received a reply to his letter. I gather he asked the academy to address its response to his trusted man in St Petersburg, who is to ensure that troops get to the cave. Of course, now there is nothing to show here and Moltique and his ape theory will become a laughing stock. Unless he were then to reveal to the press and the academy and the whole learned world that he has found a pack of werewolves! Despite Moltique's assurances, I cannot believe that any educated person will swallow claims about werewolves or centaurs just like that, in this day and age. Some of us are developing self-propelling wagons and talking of lights that do not require fire (so I heard during our journey). This does not mean the children will fare any better – the opposite, I fear: if the gutter press, along with tricksters and other adventurers seeking shock and sensation, take an interest in the cave, instead of scholars, the children's fate is sealed.

I sat there, deep in thought, and so failed to notice that Anna had also come to the brook to have a wash. I only came to when she slid onto a large fern. I know I should not look but could not take my eyes off her slender, lithe figure. She was golden and fair, silky and smooth, and the clear water of the brook did nothing to conceal her charms. I was about to warn her when I heard mocking laughter. One of Moltique's men was standing by the water making obscene gestures. Anna leapt out with the agility of a wild animal, snatched up the leathers she wore and disappeared into the sheltering forest –

JULY 15TH IN THE YEAR 1821

We spent the day under Moltique's shelter, where he has had a table built, along with a couple of large chairs and a hearth. The fire was not needed today, because it was so warm that we all stayed in the shade, trying to expend as little effort as possible on our activities. Moltique did not spare me, instead getting me to write down all the scientists he knew who had dealt with the mutations of organisms in nature.

'Comte de Buffon and Monsieur Cuvier,' he began. 'One is dead and the other is an old fool these days.' He racked his brain before telling me to note down the following publications: *Histoire naturelle* and *Leçons d'anatomie comparée*.

Then he launched into an extraordinary monologue that was packed with arguments and counterarguments. I tried to make out what I was expected to note down and what I could leave out. He added Lamarck's *Philosophie zoologique* to his bibliography, mumbled to himself for a moment, then turned to look at me, raising a finger. 'But,' he said emphatically, 'unlike that idiot Lamarck, who believes that acquired traits are inherited, I hold that things happen more randomly in nature and the world. Witchcraft, magic, miracles and chaos – unprejudiced examination of these phenomena gives rise to real science.'

I was aware that though many considered Moltique a trite windbag, there were others who deemed him a pioneering, unbiased researcher. Ordinarily, I would be able to aid him dispassionately despite my own possible doubts. But I have a personal problem: the children of the cave are important to me in a different way – as human beings, not research subjects.

Truly, the turmoil in my mind is making my body sick.

JULY 22ND IN THE YEAR 1821

I was napping when I heard shouting coming from the camp. Once out, I saw Yves lying on the ground, bleeding. He was roaring so loudly that I suspected he was not in real trouble. Others, however, were taken in by Yves's performance; the group of men appeared agitated. By the time I got to the scene, they were already thundering towards the forest, but Moltique's shout halted them. I eventually gathered that the men were demanding revenge on the children of the cave, one of whom, a sharp-toothed boy, had attacked Yves, biting him in both calves and one buttock and scratching him on the back. The injuries looked bad, but I felt no sympathy for Yves, suspecting he had somehow provoked the assault himself. Yves has the face of an angel and the nature of the Devil. I do not trust him and fear that he will succeed in inciting the men to harm the children. The rest of the day in camp was spent in an uneasy atmosphere. I fear the worst. I dare not go to sleep, though the drunken men have finally gone quiet, from the sound of it. I keep expecting one or more of their number to get up and leave with evil intent. I am ashamed of my tears. They prove the sad fact of my powerlessness, and its cause: I am a mere boy, far from home. I hate and despise myself.

JULY 23RD IN THE YEAR 1821

I would like to warn Anna, but I cannot find her anywhere –

Entries for the end of July are missing from the diary. The next entry is from August. Yves's rabies erupted some twenty days after contagion, typically for the disease.

AUGUST — IN THE YEAR 1821

Yves is in a bad way and we have hidden him from the other men. He is agitated and given to convulsions. He suffers from headache and fever, and throws up everything he eats. Rufin shakes his head, red in the face and sweating, because, despite everything, he is a real doctor at heart and feels powerless confronted by an illness that will inevitably lead to death. He has managed to convince Moltique that it is an infection caused by the bite of a sick animal, not a curse or magic. I have in the past admired the professor's open-mindedness in the face of the unknown, but now it seems more like an obsession.

Last night, I dreamed that my father and Moltique were discussing the ancient gods. Moltique claimed he had been married to Pallas Athene herself, and when my father did not believe him, he bit my father and changed him into a pig. Even as a pig, my father remained serenely gentle. He asked Moltique to leave his study so he could read in peace. If I miss anything in this godforsaken forest, here among lunatics and criminals, it is faith in the permanence of things.

AUGUST – IN THE YEAR 1821

Yves left us early this morning. I did not like him as a man, but I would have wanted his death to be less painful. If I am honest with myself, I am above all relieved that he did not get to cause greater damage. He was a rabble-rousing troublemaker. I wonder what my father would say if he learned that I had wished for the death of a man – a human being – or that I truly believe that some people are born evil. If I ever get to Paris again, or to my home in Russia, will my nearest and dearest see that I am a changed man? Hardened, maybe even evil…

AUGUST 29TH IN THE YEAR 1821

I cannot find Anna anywhere. She has gone, the children likewise. I do not understand.

Going by extracts dating from September and October, Moltique found out that Agolasky had lost the children and kept the matter secret. He punished his assistant by cutting off one of the latter's fingers. The physical injury and a resultant infection undermined Agolasky's mental health. His writings are confused and highly personal, in part; we publish only a sample here in order to grant the reader an insight into Agolasky's condition and the situation in the camp.

UNDATED

A grown man. No, no. I empty my bladder, my guts onto the sheets, which have not been washed for months. My Lord, is it you? Is this why we left France, to discover the ape in ourselves? You are great and wise.

UNDATED

I have not had a woman. She who I fell in love with is half-parrot, half-human. A mongrel. And now it left me, too. I do not say 'she'.

UNDATED

I hear them talking outside my tent at night. They whisper to each other and search, just as I do. But the children have left and will not return. The spider with supernatural abilities has taken them to safety. I shall never see Anna again.

UNDATED

They are frustrated, these friends of mine, immoral men whose company I joined. I smell fear in their sweat when they glance into the dark.

OCTOBER IN THE YEAR 1821

It must be October. It was early September when Moltique discovered that I do not know where the children are. As I have said, he does not like rebelliousness. This time, the revenge was more horrible than last time. Only now am I able to stand upright and write. Thanks to Rufin, I did not die, though my maimed hand putrefied in the hot September weather. In some sick way, I also thank my generous Lord, who holds my fate in His hand, that He spared my right hand. If anything, it is better to have lost the little finger of my left hand. I heard it was dangling on a string in the middle of the camp, but flies will have fed on it by now. That's fine, laugh away, with fear in your hearts, because we are on a journey with no hope of return.

My faith is very thin.

NOVEMBER 1ST IN THE YEAR 1821

Moltique has ordered the men to comb the vicinity. The searches have yielded no results over a period of two months. I have thought about the matter from many different angles. Owing to the influence of my father's learning and my mother's clear-sightedness, I do not believe in magic powers or miracles, and so

I concluded that Anna and the children could not be far away. Therefore, I returned to the cave and, after a moment's observation, decided to step inside. The cave appeared empty and silent, but still I sat down on a rock. Once my eyes had adjusted to the November twilight, I spotted a narrow crack in the rear wall, a little like the entrance on the other side of the hill. The crack was low and narrow, but then, the occupants of the cave were small. I tried to see if I could squeeze in, but I could not get into the hole beyond, even sideways. I pushed my hand as far as I could and felt the cavity extend. Could there be another, similarly habitable cave at the other end, with drinking water?

I spent a long time in the cave, waiting and pondering, but saw nobody.

NOVEMBER 10TH IN THE YEAR 1821

Moltique is disappointed. I see him walking in a circle in the camp, not knowing what to do now the children have vanished. I wonder what he was expecting. Reinforcements from the academy, of course, but what then? The imprisonment and transportation of the children to Paris? More thorough research? Opening up skulls, drilling, measurements, samples from inside and outside? I could imagine what a shocking sight we would have been, marching into the city with the group of children, some neighing, roaring, chirping, others discoursing intelligently but, in their fur and feathers, simultaneously both beautiful and frightening. I can only imagine the hunger of the press, the zeal of Church officials and the envy of scientists over Moltique's luck. What about fraudsters, itinerants and circus owners like Popov? Oddities attracted people and people brought money. Anna, my beautiful Anna: I saw her in golden chains in a golden cage reciting poetry in her beautiful mother tongue. If only they could hide long enough. If only Moltique were to grow weary and decide to take us elsewhere, in pursuit of other marvels. Though to be honest, I am tired of marvels. Why did I want go on adventures or see the world? Now I long for nothing more ardently than dull, uneventful days with familiar people.

Anna, I know only you.

NOVEMBER 15TH IN THE YEAR 1821

Oh! I am disappointed, frightened, glad, confused, horrified.

The following diary entry confirms that the children have returned.

NOVEMBER 17TH IN THE YEAR 1821

Anna wants me to help a boy called Kasin. Kasin is just his surname. The boy never acquired a first name, apparently. He had been left at the cave mouth with a notice round his neck, which read:

> My daughter fell in love with the wrong man and got punished: this creature, whom we have not named, is living proof. I cannot do away with a live thing that looks at me with the soulful eyes of my daughter. I can only leave it here, pray for its soul if it's got one and forget everything, as I've told my daughter to do.

Anna said the letter was signed just 'Kasin'; she believed the writer to be the boy's grandfather. Anna's eyes reflected the question that I myself sought to answer: why all this suffering?

According to Anna, it was Kasin who had bitten Yves and now the boy too was afflicted by symptoms of the disease.* I did not ask why Kasin was so important to Anna. My previous experience has been that Anna has accepted her losses resignedly. But now she has come back on account of Kasin, as if remembering how one ought to behave in the world of humans. Has my intrusion into Anna's

---

* In the light of current scientific knowledge, Kasin's form of rabies appears to present a peculiar combination of the progress of the disease in humans and in animals.

and the children's lives muddled nature's own order, in which the living are more important than the dead? What else can explain the fact that the girl has voluntarily marched her troops back to the proximity of danger? To the proximity of danger, close to me? Has Anna come back because of me?

I visited the patient but could not do anything for him. Only Pierre Rufin could alleviate the boy's pain. I thought this would be only just, having heard that Yves had frightened Kasin, provoking the boy into attacking him. Anna said Yves poked the boy with a long knife, at the same time displaying the samples in the jar. Our samples, from Buutje.

I am so ashamed of myself!

NOVEMBER 18TH IN THE YEAR 1821

I cannot eat, drink, stand, sit. I shall try to find a way of getting Rufin to the cave.

NOVEMBER 19TH IN THE YEAR 1821

Rufin refused to treat Kasin. He said that his Hippocratic oath obliged him to treat people, but not animals. What stupid pedantry from a self-taught quack! I cursed him more harshly than I had anyone before, but he merely shrugged, turned his back on me and walked off. So I could only watch Kasin's painful death, together with Anna. It made me even more certain that my task was to help not the professor but these children, who only had me. And Anna.

Anna. Anna. Anna.

The following entry is undated, but was written on either November 19th or the day after.

UNDATED

Rufin told Moltique that the children had returned. Moltique invited me to see him and enquired – with seeming politeness – why he had not had word from me. I lied and said that Rufin had just beat me to it. I was about to bring Moltique this happy news.

I no longer have any respect for myself.

UNDATED

We buried Kasin. I wanted to supply a simple cross for his grave and some text. Anna told me just to forget. Kasin was at rest now.

DECEMBER 1ST IN THE YEAR 1821

In late November, it got considerably colder. Outside it is frosty, freezing. Now and then there is snow. There is something strangely fragile about the early winter days; the darkness resembles glass. I wish I could describe these frost-clad trees, the forest as silent as a cathedral.

UNDATED

Moltique called me in. His eyes were bulging, he had not shaved, tidied up his hair or washed out his mouth. I wondered if he was losing his mind. He demanded information. Had I managed to draw up a summary of everything he had said? Had I managed to find some kind of connection between the mutation of organisms and legends? Me? He was asking me, his lowly assistant? My reply did not please him. He spat at me and shouted, 'What am I going to do with these freaks, then? Just go away? Forget all about them?'

I said he could help the children. He repeated the word 'help' scathingly, before telling me to get out of his sight.

I am sure Moltique is simply mad and his discoveries are the products of an errant mind. There is no snowman.

DECEMBER 20TH IN THE YEAR 1821

We are stuck. Our research is making no progress. It is so cold that I have to concentrate all my thoughts and energy on moving, to stay warm and alive.

DECEMBER 24TH IN THE YEAR 1821

The men killed an elk and cut it up. The cook used it to prepare a tasty meal to celebrate Christmas. I ate it, listening to the men grow nostalgic and sing carols. Some recalled their families. Even the most hardened criminals have mothers. I hope they do not miss their children. I hope they have forgotten they ever gave birth to these savages. But I suspect that's not the case: I think of women yearning for the best for their children – maybe even now, though they may know better. What about the mothers of the children of the cave, and their mothers, fathers, grandmothers, grandfathers, neighbours, uncles, aunts, acquaintances – do they remember, or have they succeeded in forgetting?

I hear footsteps outside. Too light to belong to any of the men in our camp.

The following short verses are undated but fit here to describe the romantic relationship that blossomed between Agolasky and Anna. Poetry is not Agolasky's strong point, but the verses evoke his confused mind well.

I do not know why I came.
Now I know.
But I have to say no.
I do not know why I should go.

Wake me up, I have a dream.
I wake up, the dream lives on.
Do you see what I do not,
the border between reality and dream?

You are a light in darkness.
You are warmth in coldness.
You bring beauty to this ugliness.
I cannot claim it for my own.
I am only one of many,
the least significant.

THE YEAR 1822!

The year has changed. We have been on this excursion for well over two years now. Though some days crawl by painfully slowly – I am lonely and even frightened at the camp – the years have nevertheless flown past. I can barely recall what I was when I set out on this journey. I have lived an entire life during these years and feel older than my age. I think now how peculiar the human mind is. I should be sad but, despite the pain, I smile and feel a happiness in my breast that I have never before experienced. Anna and I have been meeting often, almost daily. The days slip past – what a waste. I should be pondering over Anna's and the children's future, but I prefer to enjoy every minute with them – with her! Her laughter makes me happy, her wisdom makes me more trusting and her certainty gives me the strength to endure the unendurable. The children of the cave have only two alternatives: to stay hidden or die. But we have already found them, and I do not know how to persuade the men and Moltique to forget that this place ever existed.

JANUARY – IN THE YEAR 1822

I told Anna about my mother and she said she knew others like her: people who lead normal lives despite their animal side, which they keep strictly hidden, even from their intimates. I have been dwelling on my mother's burden. My father must know, but the subject was never raised with me. Did they not trust me? Did they not want to land me with the responsibility? I wondered about the extent of my mother's animal traits and concluded they must have been few in number because she has been alive for a long time… It occurred to me that my parents might no longer be alive; I would not get word about their deaths before surfacing from here. I try not to think about the matter because it is enough that I know I caused worry to my parents by going on this senseless adventure. Maybe they wonder, as I do here in the middle of the forest, if I am dead or alive, ill or in perfect health.

JANUARY — IN THE YEAR 1822

I had another strange dream last night. My mother had expressionless yellow eyes and, when she looked at me, I could not discern her attitude. Awake, I thought about how she was in my memories: brown eyes glinting humorously and intelligently. I saw love in them even when she was telling me off for my pranks. Those cold, haunting eyes were not real, but the product of my imagination. This forest, tirelessly humming, and the men, pursuing their basest needs, are consuming my strength. I am not that same youth who set off in May 1819, eager to accompany the scientist he admired. If I could travel back in time, I would go and drum some sense into myself: aspiring to the unreachable is the road to madness!

JANUARY — IN THE YEAR 1822

Anna hopes I will secure help for all the children who live in shadows. While it is too late now for herself and the other children of the cave, she does want my stories to persuade people to keep their children even if they have mutations, and for the world to become a safe place even for those who are different.

I wonder what I can do. I could publish my story of the children. I could show what they are like:

how beautiful, how special, how able. Once again, it grieves me that I have to make do with words. Words give the reader the option of doubting my narrative, or of filtering it through their imaginations, as will inevitably happen. But even if I could draw and paint, I could be suspected of exaggeration at best, fraudulence at worst. My witnesses would not be much use either, because not one of Moltique's men would enter a magistrate's court or anywhere else the long arm of the law might reach. Moltique himself is the only one I could pin my hopes on. He would talk about the children, all right, but would present no evidence. Parading them in Paris would be far too risky, and Moltique would not consent to take them along while still lacking a theory concerning the reasons for the children's animal traits. The same goes for the specimens in jars. Moltique could not bear scientific circles mocking him for setting out to find the heirs of the Paphlagonian people and finding merely a group of freaks for whose traits he had no explanation. Particularly when he had already written to Paris about his discovery and associated ape theories! It would be much easier to return empty-handed and tell some (fabricated) tale about our wondrous adventures in north-west Russia.

I recall all the incredible tales about Moltique's adventures and his reputation for unbiased research into legends, and pity the fool I once was. How easily hoodwinked I have been!

I also wonder why the academy has failed to send anyone.

JANUARY 25TH IN THE YEAR 1822

Her mouth tastes as if she had never uttered a bad word about anyone.

JANUARY 26TH IN THE YEAR 1822

I am out of my mind and do not know where to start. I spent the morning with Anna and the children at the cave. Some of them are hibernating, others are unwell because of the cold and some have never felt better: the boy with the hairy back has grown thick, dense fur, which keeps him warm in the gales.

I have started collecting the names of the children's parents and relatives, in order, possibly, to contact them later. Or at least appeal to their consciences when I mention them in the interviews I shall give after establishing that general opinion is on the children's side. (I recognize my own naivety in hoping for this scenario, but what else can I do? Anna believes in me. My own conviction must be firm.)[*]

When I returned to the camp, Moltique was waiting for me at the end of the path. He looked frenzied, crazier than ever. He wanted to know – for once and for all, he said – what kind of information I imagined I could get out of the children and if I could link that information to any existing theories. I decided to tell him straight that I had no scientific skills. My sole talents were my mother tongue,

[*]   The list of the names of the children's parents and relatives has not been found in the academy's archives. There is reason to suspect it has been either destroyed or confiscated.

Russian, fluent French (thanks to my father) and an ability to note things down. I added that I trusted that he, the great scientist, could bind together the information that had been gathered, or at least decide what knowledge was needed to reach conclusions. For the first time during the whole of our journey he did not mock me or laugh at me. He became silent, then turned and walked away, head bowed. I remained standing in the middle of our camp till I felt the snow burning my soles.

I was about to go to bed when Moltique called me to him. He announced tersely that we were to leave the camp. He would not discuss the matter further.

I know now that I shall not be able to sleep all night. We shall go and I shall not see Anna again.

JANUARY 27TH IN THE YEAR 1822

In the middle of the night I had a desperate idea: I suggested to Moltique that we ask the academy to send someone who could draw the children of the cave. Even if we did not find an explanation for their mutations, we could at least introduce these wonderful children to the world via pictures. This might facilitate new projects and prompt a fresh excursion to the cave. We could return, better equipped, new people with us.

Moltique did not like the idea; to be precise, he did not like the idea of us needing anyone else besides himself. And that is why he put paid to the thought of drawing the children. I saw I had approached the matter from the wrong angle.

Just before he sent me packing, he snapped,
'Anyway, soon nobody will draw the wonders of
the world. They'll be immortalized by means of
light. And soon you too will be useless – a means of
writing will be invented that has no need of pen and
paper, nor even a knowledge of Russian.'

More than by his words, I was hurt by the knowledge that I would have to leave Anna.

Moltique, however, was upset only on his own
behalf, in his selfish way. As I walked out of his hut,
he muttered that the academy was no longer interested in him... I assumed his claim was prompted
by the fact that his letter had given rise to no action.
I did not want to ask if the expedition might have
got lost on the way. We are so far from civilization,
after all, that not a single man has ever strayed into
our camp.

Moltique is impossible.

A nocturnal addition: I cannot get to sleep. I am
cold. Not even wrapping myself in furs warms me
up. I am also exercised by what Moltique said about
light and image. I want to know more about how
light produces an image: is it like a shadow stick-
ing to the ground, or to stone, fabric, paper? What
attaches it? And what about details such as faces,
are they made visible? I would wish for nothing
more than to be able to carry Anna's picture against
my chest, on my chest, close to my heart!

JANUARY 28TH IN THE YEAR 1822

The men have been ordered to ready us for the
journey. They gather together a heap of necessary
things. Prolonged lassitude has become feverish enthusiasm, not like when we left Paris, but
rather humbler, more human. I almost like the
men, because for the first time they appear fragile,
emotional. I hear someone talking about his mother
and it touches me. I remember wishing that the
men's mothers had forgotten the wretched creatures
they had carried and nourished, those misbegot-
ten scoundrels. Perhaps the men cannot help it. I
wonder what scars we each carry in our souls and
bodies. For the first time in my life, I ask myself if
a criminal character might be a similar aberration
of nature to feathers or a parrot's tongue. What
about my own peculiarities, the fantasies I harbour
of pictures I can transfer onto paper with my eyes?
Illusions, fantasies, genius, a dream, or something
once heard in a Parisian tavern and mistaken for my
own invention?

Momentarily moved, I look at Simon and see a
happy smile on his face. I only ever remember him
smiling – or rather grinning lecherously – when telling mendacious tales of his non-existent adventures
with women. Now he is saying something to Cook,
hands moving about, and he throws his head back
and laughs up at the sky. In other circumstances, I
might be able to ignore his stupid tales… In other
circumstances, he might not feel the need to entertain older rogues with his repulsive lies.

I turn to look at Paul and, for a moment, I see
him as just as harmless as he is. Is he not a victim
rather than guilty – a fatherless boy, for whom
Moltique, along with his party, represented a family
of sorts, because he had no other?

I wish I had no feelings for Anna and the children. I would like to be as eager to go as the men,
who are gathering up things and dreaming of
what they will encounter on the way: drink, food,
women, people, music, cities.

But I am not about to go anywhere, though I
pretend otherwise to Moltique.

JANUARY – IN THE YEAR 1822

I was returning from Anna when I noticed I was
being followed. I heard panting, the crunching of
snow, sobbing and irritable hissing. I stopped to
wait. Soon, two very hairy little boys waded out
of the snowdrifts. I recognized them at once as the
Vodkin brothers. The smaller of them cannot speak.
His behaviour is also highly animalistic, so I do
not expect he will live very long, given what Anna
has reported. The larger of the two, by contrast, is
like anyone else, apart from a thick covering of fur
and the fact that he is unusually clever, gentle and
caring. Panting heavily, he said he knew we were
leaving. I did not know how to answer, so I told
him, in confidence, that I was staying. Contrary to
what I imagined or hoped, the information did not
calm him. It had the opposite effect, in fact: his eyes
widened and he hit me! I was so surprised that, for

a moment, I could only hold my ringing ear and tingling cheek. Then he began to cry and I was not able to challenge him over his conduct. I shifted my feet awkwardly, because the younger Vodkin was clinging to his big brother's fur so that I could not comfort his grief-stricken sibling. Finally, the boy calmed down enough to explain that he had hoped I would take his brother along with me wherever I would be going. He said he suspected that his brother might have contracted the disease that was killing children in the cave. The younger Vodkin had got mixed up in a scrap involving the most animal-like of the children. Teeth had been bared and the younger Vodkin had been bitten. Rabies. I thought of Kasin and I knew the older brother was thinking the same thing.

Come night, I once again go back on my deci-sion: I will not stay behind when the expedition departs. Instead, I will go, to return either alone or in suitable company. I will find out if anyone, in any part of the world, has studied the mutations carried by the children of the cave. It may take the rest of my life, but I do not intend to let a single child suffer as the children I know do now. I am also profoundly sad that I cannot do anything for the younger Vodkin; I only hope he reaches the end of his natural life before the rabies strikes.

JANUARY — IN THE YEAR 1822

I listen to the men talking in the dark. Fist's voice rings out again. I fear him the most. He speaks

more quietly, but even though I do not hear everything, I discern the gist: he is using foul language
about Anna. He is talking about his youthful travels
in the Rhineland, where he heard about the udder
goat, a woman who forms an alliance with the
Devil. I can almost smell the men's fear growing as
they listen to the story. They glance at the forest,
shifting restlessly and swearing. Then someone
says, perhaps Cook, that on his deathbed, Yves had
spoken of all the things he had done with the 'hairy
bitch' belonging to 'the Professor's little helper' –
that's me! The comments raise snorts and the
conversation changes direction. Apart from being
repulsed by Yves's disgusting tales, I am profoundly
saddened by the way Anna and the children are
treated. These men have no understanding of what
is beautiful or noble; their world revolves around
the region between their shit-spouting mouths
and their arseholes – and I write like this because
good manners are nothing to me now. Would my
father deny me, if he saw what had become of me?
Would I be allowed to continue using his name? The
Agolaskys – men who love peace, women who cher-
ish beauty. I no longer measure up to my name.

The hatred that burns inside me does not alleviate my fear. I shall not sleep tonight, for sure.

POSSIBLY FEBRUARY 8TH IN THE YEAR 1822

I hope we shall manage to depart before anything
happens. As if something had not already happened. How many unnecessary deaths will I yet

have to suffer? I, who imagined I could embark on adventures from behind paper and words – without feeling, experiencing, being part of...

— YEAR 1822

This I want to remember for ever: Anna said I am the best thing that ever happened to her. She said that I am a good man and I should not doubt that. She told me not to grieve, even if we were never to meet again. I asked her what she meant. She would not reply, instead calling out instructions to the little ones in order to avoid my question. I never met anyone as adept at evading questions. I swore to her that I would come back. She kissed me, stroked my head and said that was exactly why she liked me. Why?

— IN THE YEAR 1822

– the dawn came. At last. I can't see anyone outside. Who or what was it, and what did it want from me? I feel eyes on my back as I walk across the camp. Moltique –

FEBRUARY — IN THE YEAR 1822

Everything is going wrong. We should already be –

FEBRUARY — IN THE YEAR 1822

I do not understand –

This section of the notes has been destroyed, or else Agolasky simply did not write it. The following entry makes clear that Moltique was inexplicably missing for a time.

Since his return, Moltique has been growing more and more unpredictable. The men give him a wide berth. I only go to him if I have to. No one dares ask if we are leaving the camp and, if so, when. And where? Back to Paris?

Something very odd happened today. Moltique dictated to me and I wrote down everything obediently, though his thoughts were ricocheting crazily between zoologists' theories and folk tales. The only connecting factor was a creature that was half-man, half-animal. Our great researcher had collided with a reality that he could not explain. I wondered if Moltique had tried to explain the snowman or if it was enough for him that he had seen it.* I was deep in thought and did not immediately notice what

---

* Agolasky did not know that some parties critical of Moltique's professional abilities in the academy had mocked him throughout his career for only being able to make observations, not interpret the phenomena he reported seeing. Academy records mention an incident during which one researcher had vilified Moltique rather harshly: 'Professor Moltique is a windbag who offers up only scandals and popular entertainment. His capacity for scientific thought is as developed as that of an ape.' Discovering the children of the cave had most likely appeared to Moltique to offer an opportunity to prove to his critics that he was a wide-ranging and estimable researcher – this would explain his obsession with the task.

Moltique was doing. Suddenly, I came to, alerted
by his silence. He was sniffing the air suspiciously.
I asked what he thought he could smell, but he
failed to reply. Snow smelt different in early spring,
sweeter, than earlier in winter – that was all. I did
not sense anything else myself. But Moltique was
sniffing the air eagerly, head thrown back, eyes half-
closed. Then – out of the blue – he stopped smell-
ing, nailed me with his angry eyes and told me to
get lost. I was more than happy to leave.

MARCH 16TH IN THE YEAR 1822

I woke up very early this morning – about an hour
ago – because I heard someone moving outside. I
put on my coat and went out. It was still dark and
I couldn't see anything. Then I spied a largish creature close to Moltique's quarters. At first I thought
it was a bear, but it was too small. Then I thought it
might well be a wolf come to root among our left-
overs. Something about the creature's movements
made me stay on the spot, observing for longer. As
my eyes adjusted to the dark, I saw it did not move
with animal agility but like a man, crawling around.

I went to get a lantern, which I lit. Then I started
cautiously towards the figure. Step by step, I
approached it, alert and ready to flee if the creature
straying into our camp proved to be a wild animal.
I heard snuffling, growling and strange suckling
noises, then saw, in the light of my lantern… a
pair of bare soles. They belonged not to an animal
of north-west Russia but to Professor Moltique.

I stopped, frozen to the spot, and did not utter a word. I observed the bizarre sight spellbound: with the frenzy of a hungry animal, Moltique was tearing into the remnants of a dead hare that had been flung into the fire. He was in his pyjamas, on his knees, in the snow, hands purple, face greasy, a wild glint in his eyes. And then – he looked up at me and I knew. I was quite sure. Our expedition was doomed. The fates of Anna, the children and myself were all in the hands of a group of dishonourable men and an unhinged professor.

I turned and ran to my shelter. I flung myself onto my bunk and cried. By the time I had stopped, it was deserted outside. Moltique had gone back to bed – or else run into the forest.

MARCH 20TH IN THE YEAR 1822

I have not told Anna about Moltique. Perhaps because I am frightened. An idea has crept into my head: our forest is bewitched. The children's best protection is that all those who come here change into animals, one by one. No, I do not believe it myself. The real reason is more likely to be that all this time I have feared for the children. Not so much on account of Moltique – it's the other men I worry about. Now that Moltique appears to be mentally ill, I am even more frightened about what they may do to the children. How can I convince them that the children have nothing to do with the great, awe-inspiring professor who recruited them for the expedition regressing to the level of an animal?

Today Anna asked what was troubling me. I did not reply. But I think they all sense my increasing worry on their behalf.

MARCH 22ND IN THE YEAR 1822

I was on my way back to the camp from the privy when Paul appeared from behind some boulders and asked to speak to me in confidence. We waded one after the other in the thawing, collapsing snow, deeper into the forest, then stopped to face each other. I had never before looked him straight in the eye, man to man. We stood for a moment in awkward silence, because Paul recalls as clearly as I do what they have done to me. He collected himself, however, and said he was worried. No, that wasn't the word he used. It was afraid. He was afraid. He asked if I knew what was wrong with the professor. Wrong? I thought. What was wrong with all of us? It was as if he were talking about gout, or a bad tooth, or a headache, or woman trouble, though I could see he was on the verge of tears, in fear of his life. Paul seemed surprised when I exploded into laughter. My laughter was loud and shrill, because I was furious. If I were a different man, I would have smashed the wretched coward's face in, on behalf of myself and all the dead children. To give the man his due, he restrained himself and waited for me to calm down. I seem to be the only one in camp whom he trusts in this situation. He is, after all, one of the most harmless ones, a mere miserable boy, a poor man's orphan. Writing this now, I cannot

help but wonder what he has experienced in his life,
though he has hardly any beard on his smooth chin.

After I had calmed down, I said – straight and
unadorned – that I suspected Moltique had lost
the light of his reason; to speak plainly, that he was
mad and in his darkest moments imagined he was
some kind of animal. This information had the
desired effect on Paul: his face drained of colour
and his lips started trembling. I saw tears welling up
in his brown eyes again – goodness and lost dignity
shone out from them – and finally he began sobbing. He begged me for advice: what should he do?
Follow Moltique's gang, was that the only option?
I said that was all we could do if we wanted to get
back to civilization alive, out of the wilderness.
That made Paul reveal something I had been desperate to know since the start of the conversation. He
is afraid of Fist, who has decided to slaughter the
most human of the children of the cave, capture the
rest, and also kill Moltique and myself if we object.
Cook and Fist intend to cash in on parading the
remains of the dead children, along with the most
animal-like specimens, whom they will allow to
survive. Somehow, I knew all this but I am still horrified by the wickedness and grotesqueness of the
plan, as well as by its short-sightedness. The most
animal-like children do not live long to begin with
and in captivity, transported round Europe, they
would be certain not to last –

I wondered who and what Cook was before
he joined us. He claims to have hidden a cache
of money in Paris, on which he will live when he

returns to the city. But he is probably as desperate as the other men and as lacking in cash. What will they do for a living when we get back? Could I make them believe that, if they stick with me (and Moltique), their future is secure?

— IN THE YEAR 1822

I grew up in a cultured family. My friends were the healthy children of scholars and landowners. I am sure to be the only one who left family-owned land, an ancestral estate, behind them. Now I am following a mad professor somewhere on the border between Finland and Russia; my love is a martyr abandoned by her family, more courageous than Joan of Arc, disabled as she is; and my best friend is a duplicitous minor criminal, a youth somewhere between a street perfomer and a pickpocket who has tortured and tormented me. We have a common objective, however: to make Moltique appear confident and authoritative, a leader whose feet and head both still function, and so to prevent an unnecessary bloodbath.

The children must be hidden.

MARCH 23RD IN THE YEAR 1822

My first act was to lie to the men and say Moltique was setting up a research station at the cave. They would all get well-paid jobs and respectable positions there. They could forget their pasts, change their names and reputations and start their whole lives over. I do not know if they believed me. Moltique is missing again; I claimed he was involved in fieldwork at the cave. At least he is not howling in his cabin and will not rush over to nibble my calves… I may gain a couple of extra days.

I have to get to the cave.

Added at night: I could not find Anna. I did not see the professor. I did not –

MARCH 24TH IN THE YEAR 1822

Where are you, Anna? Where have you gone? I miss you, but do stay away. Do not appear again unexpectedly, do not walk straight into a trap set by Cook and Fist.

My God, I beseech you.

MARCH 25TH IN THE YEAR 1822

I am cold, but no matter. It is early morning. I have just come back from the forest. Once the men had fallen asleep and the camp had quietened, I slipped to the cave. I crouched outside for a long time and thought back to those days two years ago: then, observing the cave was spellbinding and exciting; this time, I was eaten up by fear. Then, I waited eagerly for a glimpse of the children; now, I hoped they would stay away.

I was about to leave the cave when I spotted Professor Moltique. He ran, half-crouching, among the trees, sank into the thawing snow, stumbled, fell, got up again and went on with his clumsy effort at running. I watched the professor I once admired with a mixture of pity and fury. I saw the unbearable grotesqueness of his abasement, but recalled his unpredictability and nasty superciliousness. I despised myself for having respected him and kowtowed to him so willingly, and yet my heart was gripped by a deep sadness as I watched his inevitable decline.

As I watched, Moltique knelt in the wet snow and started for the cave mouth. He sniffed the ground, occasionally lifting his face and emitting an odd, squeaking sound. I thought it just as well I did not have a gun. I, who have never felt the need to kill any living creature!

Moltique reached the entrance and vanished into the darkness. I waited a long time, eventually becoming worried, but finally he came back. He lowered his trousers – he has retained that much humanity – and emptied his bladder like a dog, with one leg raised, in front of the cave. Not even the most animalistic of the cave children are that ill-mannered: they all go to the toilet at a decent distance from their dwelling, just as we and our gang of criminals have set up our latrine outside the camp. How low will Moltique yet sink?

I turned and started back for camp, trembling with disgust. I had only taken a few steps when I bumped into Cook, leaning against a pine by the path we had trampled into the ground. He looked at me strangely, asking why I was out at night. I said I was trying to find Moltique. Cook asked if I had done so and I lied, saying there was no sign of the professor. He repeated the words 'no sign' after me, peering over my shoulder at the cave. Did he see what I did – Moltique crawling on the ground? If he did, what conclusion did Cook, and Fist, come to?

Many pages of the book appear to have been destroyed at this point. The following extracts are undated, but their contents indicate they should be placed here, given the course of events.

— IN THE YEAR 1822

I dreamed of a massacre. In the dream, Anna was sitting among dead children, singing the lullaby my mother used to sing to me.

— IN THE YEAR 1822

Moltique has returned. He is having a better day today, acting as if nothing has happened and appearing fairly normal. He called me in to him first thing, wanting me to go through our notes. They seemed embarrassingly muddled to me, but the professor listened seriously, nodding sagely. I do not think he actually listened to my halting reading. He seems to be in pain and his hands are in a terrible state. He froze them badly while crawling in the snow: the joints of his fingers are red and swollen, the skin is all shiny and dotted with protuberances secreting fluid. He does not wear shoes, but pads about in oversized felt boots, which makes me suspect his feet are also in a bad state.

After I had finished reading the notes, Moltique asked how preparations for our departure were progressing. I did not dare ask if we were leaving. Matters seemed settled to him. He clarified: the men knew what to do? I nodded; I could not disclose that if the men's whole time and resources did not go on staying alive – hunting, fetching water and wood, making fires, cooking and repairing utensils – the consequences would be fatal. The camp is already teeming with activity: Fist and Cook are working out whom to trust and whom to get rid of, when the time is right. Some of the men believed my lie about founding a research station and the jobs this will provide. I can't bear to think about what will happen if my lie is exposed.

Fortunately, Moltique did not wonder why I did not reply. Instead, he uttered his first sensible sentence during our whole excursion: 'I cannot solve this riddle. I don't know enough. We'll go back to Paris and get hold of the right people. Not that I care one iota about the fate of these children, but I want to know if regressing to an animal is becoming more common. Could it affect any of us?' I looked at him, struck by the grotesqueness of the idea. He, a wolf in man's clothing.

As I write this, worry gnaws at my breast. What will happen if Moltique calls a camp meeting tomorrow and asks about preparations for departure?

Added at night: I woke up from a restless sleep. I write to achieve some kind of peace. I have been wondering where Anna will take the children. She has not told me and I have not asked. If someone enquired, I would not want to have the secret extracted from me against my will. I do not even know if their refuge will provide shelter for a longer period or if Anna will have to return to the cave at some point. Today, I saw footprints outside the cave; they told me someone had been there. Anna? Fist? Cook? Moltique? One of the children? I also wondered if Anna missed me.

APRIL 9TH IN THE YEAR 1822

I cannot concentrate. When I cross the camp, I imagine the men looking at me ominously.

APRIL 10TH IN THE YEAR 1822

Luck is on my side. Awful to say this when some of Professor Moltique's frozen fingers have developed gangrene. But the professor's extremely poor health provides me with brief respite. I asked Pierre Rufin if Moltique would recover, but he did not dare promise me anything one way or the other.

APRIL — IN THE YEAR 1822

Fist and Cook have taken control. Neither of them pretends otherwise. They have set the men to work preparing for the journey and incited dogs to track the children. The atmosphere in the camp is feverish. The men, who believed my lies about the research station, are sullen but do what Fist and Cook want. I enquired discreetly what they think and learned most believe Moltique will die. What will happen to the research station if we no longer

have a leader? they ask. Obviously, they do not
consider me a serious leadership candidate. I cannot
blame them. I am young, wretched, frightened.

APRIL — IN THE YEAR 1822

I returned to the camp a moment ago from a visit
to the cave. It was quiet, and there was no indica-
tion that Anna and the children had returned. I felt
relieved. Still, the fear that they might walk straight
into Fist's trap drove me to despair. I sat on a stone
nearby and burst into tears – I, a grown man. I do
not seem able to control myself but sob like a child
at the slightest emotion. Crying, I began to sense
that I was not alone. As if, while living in the forest,
I had acquired a new instinct that would enable
me to detect a human standing silently a couple of
metres away. I grew quiet and calmed myself down.
I listened. A shape like a human being had appeared
in the silence of the surrounding nature. My hackles
rose, my ears twitched and my mouth twisted into a
grin; I was ready to fight for my life. Then a barely
discernible, familiar sound, a sigh perhaps, soothed
me. My heart went on galloping wildly, but for
other reasons.

I whispered Anna's name. No reply. I added my
name, I said it was me, and only then did she dare
answer. Her voice sounded small and tired. She said
she would not come to me, but instead stay in the
dark. I understood her: as a child, if I were frightened in the forest, the darkness would serve as a
blanket to wrap around myself.

I asked how they were. Anna said she was fine, but the younger of the Vodkins was ill and would soon die. The elder brother was heartbroken. The news pierced my heart. I thought of the pair, recalling the insistence with which the elder Vodkin had demanded I seek help for the younger. Too late now. I comforted Anna, promising to return. I made her swear she would stay hidden. She said they would not return to the cave until after our departure.

Several pages are again missing from Agolasky's diary. The story about The Spider seems to have been penned by Agolasky and could have been written at a time of confusion in the camp, while Moltique was ill and Fist was growing in dominance and looking for Anna and the children.

THE SPIDER

Once upon a time, far away, in the middle of a forest, there was a cave inhabited by a group of unusual children, and probably it is still there today. Some of them could see in the dark, navigate with their hearing or identify danger by smell alone. Some of them had fur that changed colour in winter, or grew limbs to replace damaged ones, or varied hue to match their surroundings. They were astonishingly fine evidence of the capacity of nature to transform and mould a creature in accordance with the requirements of the environment. Some of the same children could play a melody by ear, draw what they saw and speak many tongues. In the forest, nobody asked them to play or draw or speak many tongues. They had been brought there and forgotten about.

These magnificent children, different in different ways, had one thing in common: none had a family – no father, no mother, nor any other relatives. They had only each other – and a girl called Anna, who was as beautiful as a fairy, as brave as a soldier, as magnanimous as a prince and as wise as all three Magi from the Orient: Caspar, Melchior and Balthazar, all put together. But still, she was only a girl, a girl so small that anyone could throw her down, walk over her clad in boots, crush and abandon her. These children and the wicked world, and this girl in between, a fragile wall, a delicate guard. Because of a shortage of strength, cunning was needed in compensation. The girl remained alert, and she emphasized alertness to the other children, and when danger threatened, they fled and hid in the shadows. In the dark, hidden from light and eyes, they were safe; as long they were not visible, they could not be harmed. The main thing was to be still and silent. Panic and fear reduced their chances of survival – a single false move or reckless act could imperil them all. Living in fear is hard; it ages you rapidly. In the civilized world, people rely if not on each other then on God. The children of the cave either had not heard of God or, if they had, did not consider Him a significant source of support. You could not blame them; those who abandoned them at the cave mouth talked about God, prayed to God, blamed God or cursed Him. God did not greatly impress the children of the cave. But fortunately, there was The Spider.

Everyone knew that The Spider was one of them. He, too, had spent his childhood in a cave, grown up, developed and finally left. He travelled round the world to rescue the weak and the downtrodden. It was said that when he encountered evil, he was ruthless. The Spider walked, ran, jumped and climbed at breakneck speed; he was able to scale vertical walls and hang upside down with equal facility. His hands and feet – eight in number – had sharp nails which enabled him to cling to any surface. With his webs, he could cover long distances, cross abysses and fords and drop down safely on his target. In short, The Spider was supreme in his cunning and vindictiveness. The Spider also had poison glands. By deploying the stingers on his chin, he could paralyse his victim, wrap it in his web and leave it to die.

In times of greatest trouble and despair – as now, hiding from wicked men who had strayed into the forest – the children derived strength from The Spider. They relished the thought of him coming, to leap from a branch on top of the men with his sticky web, wrapping them up in tight parcels and leaving them to kick. When the last of the baddies was too tired and thirsty to call or even whisper for help, too exhausted to move a muscle and too desperate even to cry, The Spider walked out of the forest on its four hairy legs – and whispered... The men in the web pricked up their ears. What did it say? they slurred, tongues dry with terror. What did it say?

The Spider said: I'm hungry.

MAY 1ST IN THE YEAR 1822

Today I visited Moltique. He was lying with his eyes closed. Both hands and feet were wrapped in grey bandages, which I knew Rufin had torn off our sheets and boiled before use. He was doing his best, but Moltique looked as if he were dying rather than recovering. His face was sweaty and pallid, and his colourless lips were moving. I bent closer to hear his words. He spoke rapidly and indistinctly, and in such a weak voice that it was hard to tell what language he was using. He smelt bad, sweet and sour at the same time, and I was disgusted by the white froth that had dried round his mouth. I sank into my thoughts for a moment and did not notice Moltique opening his eyes. He looked at me, pupils enlarged, nostrils twitching. He groaned, 'I am a crocodile who dwells in terror, I am a sacred crocodile, I destroy.'* Then he croaked and sank back into his stupor, which would be his end, or a new beginning.

MAY — IN THE YEAR 1822

The weather has quickly become more temper-
ate and now feels almost summery. Nature is still
new and there is something still innocent about
the leaves of the trees, greenery that does not yet

---

*   Moltique was citing the *Book of the Dead*, also known as the 'Papyrus of Ani', part of the so-called Theban texts. This was discovered in Thebes only in 1888. Researchers have wondered how it was possible for Moltique to be familiar with the texts in 1822, two years before the French researcher Jean-François Champollion published his *Précis du système hiéroglyphique des anciens Égyptiens* – and as much as sixty-seven years before the 'Papyrus of Ani' was discovered. It is known that Moltique's circle of friends and admirers included some of the major Egyptologists of the time, but there is no record of a trip by Moltique to Egypt. It is a pity that Agolasky was not able to wonder at Moltique's knowledge; it might have made him have faith in this unique and frightening employer, whom Agolasky regarded only as a wretched fraudster for the rest of his days. The allusion to the *Book of the Dead* demonstrates that Moltique had travelled further and wider than anyone knew and that he had collected information from different fields without bias. Maybe his claim about the snowman was also true.

know it is green. The ground is white with wood
anemones; marsh marigolds flower by the brook.
But this paradise contains a snake with the head of
Cook and the body of Fist. Those two are working
tirelessly to find the children and, after a day with
no luck, they grow angrier and more venomous.
Paul and I try to meet, so I can learn what the men
talk about among themselves. I know I am being
followed: the men think I shall lead them to the
children. I do not know how long they will have
the energy to continue this nerve-racking game of
hide-and-seek, and what will happen if Anna is
more cunning than they. I am struck by a horrible
thought, and I hope Fist will not have the same
idea: what if they decide to use me as bait? To tie
me, battered, somewhere close to the cave? I force
myself to think of something else, because fear
gnaws at me the same way gangrene is destroying
Moltique's body.

I hope to know more once I have met Paul.

MAY 27TH IN THE YEAR 1822

Night again. A northern spring night, pale and
clear, like milk diluted with water. At a different
moment, in a different life, this night would play
upon my soul. I recall distantly what it feels like
to be happy. The memory blinks in my mind and
then vanishes. Nostalgia rises like mist upon the
nearby marsh. In the silence of my quarters, I shiver
and sweat, cry and laugh. I say farewell to myself.
Farewell to myself as I am today, and as I was

before. I know now I shall not survive this adventure. I do not matter. I am only sorry that I shall have to see Cook and Fist assaulting Anna and the children, killing those of no use to them and capturing those they intend to transport to Paris. I have no reason to doubt Paul's information.

Paul has disappeared. I have been so deep in my thoughts that I have only just noticed his absence. I went round the whole camp today, asking everyone where he was, and he is definitely not here. I wonder what could have happened to him; I fear that Cook and Fist have forced him to talk. It would not take a lot. Even at their most benign, they are frightening, and Paul, for his part, is a big-mouthed sycophant and a coward to boot. If Paul has blabbed, Cook and Fist will know that I have misled the men with my tall tales of a research station and keeping Moltique's condition secret. They'll know I have warned Anna and the children. And they'll no doubt imagine I am trying to turn other men than Paul against them. Put simply, I am an enemy. There is only one thing for it: hide.

I am unclear about the date. It is June, I know that much. I fled the camp six or seven or even eight nights ago; I have lost count. I do not know if single days or nights even have any meaning any more.

The sun rises, the sun sets, flowers open, flowers close, for a while the day-birds sing and then it is the turn of the night-birds. Nobody in nature counts the days, weeks, months, years, the defeats or the victories. There is only one reason to exist: life itself.

I cannot sleep, but on occasions, when awake, I notice I have fallen into a state you could call sleep. During those states, I ponder over the past and the future, right and wrong, big questions, people who are close to me but far away, and distant people close to me. I do not feel rested after these spells, but rather refreshed in a strange, excited way.

I think it is a new day. I fell asleep in the early evening and when I woke up it was light. I decided to take some exercise. I dare not walk long distances because I am afraid of getting lost and not being able to find the way to the camp or the cave. Though I do not know when I will venture back. Shall I ever? And what will happen if I do return? And what will become of me if I do not return? The uncertainty and indecision are vexing me. I am like an imbecile, I rave, I talk to myself and I vomit frequently. I have stomach ache and, though my provisions are running low, I cannot muster up any worry about my nourishment; I do not feel hunger. My mouth is permanently dry and I can feel my lips bleeding.

I woke up. Is it a new day or am I in the previous one? I observe a diligent bird carrying food to its nest. Incessant chirping emanates from the creature. Birds are wiser than humans. They do not desire fame or glory, they do not seek adventures, nor do they find danger appealing. The main thing is to stay alive.

These entries are written in shaky, near-illegible hand-writing; the last ones are mere scrawls on the paper. There are mysterious drawings next to them.

I woke up again. Though I am not sure if I did fall asleep. The sun warms me like a large, hot hand.

I woke up, but it is night or a dark day.

I woke up. I am lonely.

I woke up. I am getting tired.

I woke up. I have to count.

I woke up. Nausea.

– light fire soft cold peace father mother apple trees anna my anna come lips I faithful
Noir are you alive still

?

I wko

I wkoed

I wo

JULY IN THE YEAR 1822

Anna presumes it is July. She does not keep a record of the days or the months. The years will pass, in any case, she says, but going by my diary, she is confident that the month has changed. July must be well advanced because willowherb is flowering by the forest. In my memories, willowherb blossoms at the point in summer when we return home from our dacha. It is nearly harvest time. I am sitting in a cart next to my mother, wearing a cap and a scarf; with us is a young crow I tamed at the dacha. It comes when I call its name – Vasili – and bows when I give it a piece of bread. Was I happy then? Was I even me? It is as if my past belonged to someone else. Who is this nine-fingered man who has retained his boyhood but lost his childish faith? Who is this bearded, sickly savage that I have become? This coward, running away from a wild bunch of petty criminals, hiding among children in the depths of a forest? This wretched, shivering, malodorous good-for-nothing, whom his own parents would not recognize? Who am I?

Anna says: you're Iax. You're my life. You're the only one I've ever loved.

She found me in the forest. I was raving, trembling, ill. I would have died without her. I do not understand why I had not eaten or drunk, why I had drifted into a state in which I could not make decisions. Finally, I was too weak. I wonder if Moltique is still alive.

JULY/AUGUST IN THE YEAR 1822

Yesterday, we found Paul.

Today, I shall burn his name on a piece of dried wood that I found. I plan to place it on his grave, a miserable hole in peatland, deep in the forest. I only know Paul's forename and the year of his death; I believe he was born in France, but I do not know his age. Perhaps I am the only one left behind who misses him.

As I contemplated Paul and his fate, it occurred to me that love and hate, fear and hope are not opposite emotions. Like sunlight: you see shadow in a forest, bright sunshine in an open field, but the cause is the same. Paul was my shadow and my sunshine. Though I hated and detested him as he spat on me and grinned at my pain – Moltique's punishment for my treachery – I still trusted him enough to ally myself with him. Now that he is absent, I mourn his unhappy fate. His death was slow and painful.

I wonder what Cook and Fist are doing. The wilderness is boundless. Will they persist in looking for me? Do they think they will find me?

AUGUST IN THE YEAR 1822

For the first time, I have the opportunity to observe Anna's and the children's lives close up. I note that the children of the cave have divided themselves according to their characteristics. The most human of them spend time together; they decide on things

and take care of the others. The friendly, sociable children frolic close to them; they understand
simple rules and commands. The wildest and most
unpredictable of the children like their own company, clashing occasionally. Then Anna, Katya or
Nikolai get involved before anything very serious
happens. Still, small injuries are unavoidable. Every
now and then, someone gets pushed off a ledge,
or someone is hit, bitten or strangled. Illness and
death are routine among the children. I notice that
not even the most human among them plans for
the future, something that is otherwise routine in
our society. Anna does not dream of a life outside
the cave, either. She does not think about ageing, or
how the children of the cave would manage if anything happened to her. She lives in the cave today,
here and now. How different we are.

One day, we were lying in a sheltered place close
to our cave. I was chewing a stalk of grass and the
situation suddenly evoked another one, from my
previous life, to such an extent that I forgot where
I was. So I turned to Anna, relaxed, and placed my
hand on her stomach. I realized I let slip an inanity
that did not fit with our reality. I said to Anna that
I wanted a child with her. First, she stiffened. Then
she removed my hand, sat up, turned her head and
killed my suggestion stone-dead with her silence.
How could I? I said I was sorry. I laughed. I said the
sun must have gone to my head. And Anna. Anna
was acting as if she could no longer hear my voice. I
left her, embarrassed, shaken, hollow.

The following entries are undated. Agolasky appears to have given up trying to establish precise dates.

Let it be September. Touches of yellow in the trees. I have lost my sense of time, my past and my future. I have only the present.

I play with Katya. I hide in the dark cave; time after time, she finds me. She says I smell sweet, like rotten fruit, and at the same time pungent, like autumnal soil. She does not say it in a spirit of criticism, but I am glad I cannot smell myself. Dirt covers me, garment-like. My clothes are beginning to disintegrate. My trousers split at the knees when I bent over today. My shirt is torn at the armpits, the buttons are missing. How does a human cope without clothes?

Roberto the Lion King sat next to me by the fire. He wanted to discuss the world outside the cave. He said he was bored and longed for adventures. I, in turn, said I was tired of adventures. He laughed and poked me with his elbow; he did not believe a word of it. Then he, the hairy Tom Thumb, stood up on a rock, thumped his chest with his fists and shouted out that he yearned for excitement. I thought of Cook and Fist and the excitement they could provide us.

I surprised Nikolai today licking his leg. It was
wounded. I asked if he wanted help and he merely
shook his head, smiling. How could I help him?
He is stronger, more cunning and capable than
I. He has also grown; when he stood up, I saw he
was taller than I. His fur-covered chest has become
broader, too. He is no longer a boy, but a man. To
cap it all, he is clever. I caught myself thinking he
would be the perfect partner for Anna. I was stung
by jealousy, I must admit. Suddenly I felt both old
and weak. An unprepossessing male.

The boy called Durak sits on a ledge at the back
of the cave by day. He puts his arms round himself, closes his eyes and rocks himself to sleep. I
asked Anna to tell me about his background. Anna
shrugged, smiled sadly and said it was the same
old story. Durak was born covered with feathers,
abandoned by the road in a basket and picked
up by a strange old man, who reared him in his
peculiar zoo. When the man died, the animals
starved to death in their cages and pens, but Durak
managed to escape. Anna extracted this tale from
Durak over a long period. He does not like talking; also, his speech is poor, and were it not for the
old man's little girl, he might never have learned
to speak. She spent hours by Durak's cage, telling
stories about her miserable life. She also recounted
what she had heard about Durak from her father.
The basket in which he had been placed as a baby
was quite ordinary, but the animal fur he had been
wrapped in was very fine and the man had been

able to sell it for quite a bit of money. I wondered who among the nobility of my homeland had given birth to a feather-covered baby and was capable of leaving it by the road at the mercy of wolves and robbers. I also wondered what happened to the little girl in the story. And how Durak had ended up among the children of shadows, deep in the forest.

At night, Durak climbs down from the ledge and goes hunting. He returns with moles and mice tucked under his belt – these he skins deftly to eat for his evening snack. He is ominous, somehow, in his silence. I also abhor his way of twisting his head and looking at the rest of us from his height, where he lives like a hermit. Poor people, him and me. All of us.

I like to sleep with the children who gather together at night. Their breathing is calm and even. They trust the darkness of the cave; they feel safe in it. I cannot get to sleep myself. I am startled by cracks coming from the forest. I dream of Cook and Fist approaching the cave with torches, armed with sabres, swords and carbines. Their minds are poisoned with terrifying stories and, in their view, they are tasked with performing a service to the whole civilized world. They have forgotten only one thing: they themselves are outside the civilized world. But they do not hesitate to obey the order. Torchlight glints in their unfeeling eyes. They are bloodthirsty and vengeful. Humiliation is their pleasure.

I have nightmares in which Fist sits on me, capturing me between his strong thighs. Then he – I wake up from the dreams soaking and feeling sick. Fear gnaws away at my humanity.

Today I was walking in a nearby clearing. I saw deer, hares and a stoat. The sun was shining and I allowed myself to sit by a rock, in its heat. Suddenly, I was roused by the certainty of being observed from the forest. I leapt up, seized by a cold terror. I was more afraid than perhaps ever before on this trip that has turned into a nightmare and I began to run as fast as I could, away from the cave. I ran until I tasted blood in my mouth and my lungs were stinging. I fell and couldn't get up. I heard the forest rumbling as the group of men approached. They were panting and swearing. The ground trembled – they would find me soon. But once my breath had steadied, I heard only the usual forest noises: birds, branches snapping and a light breeze. I was alone and lost. It was night-time before I found my way back to the cave. I did not want to go in and frighten the children. I hid outside in a small depression and curled up to try and get warm. Anna found me in the morning. Now I am drinking hot water, which she has brought to alleviate my ague.

Anna watching me, thinking I am unaware of her gaze. What could be stirring behind those thoughtful eyes? How does she perceive me?

She touched me today. Her hand was light and comforting. Before I had time to say anything, she turned her back and –

I understand her. Her life is in the cave and with these children. Come what may. I am an outsider.

SEPTEMBER, MAYBE OCTOBER IN THE YEAR 1822

I have no ink left. I see this as a sign of some kind. I have been running away for too long and have eschewed making decisions. When I encountered the bottom of the ink bottle I had brought from camp, I woke up to my abasement. I am no help in the cave, but rather a hindrance, because through ineptitude I led Cook and Fist to the children's hideaway.

I think it is now the end of September, or perhaps we are into October. The weather has become variable, the trees have begun to shed their leaves and an iron smell, harbinger of death, rises from nature. I shiver in my tattered clothes. My concern about Anna and the children grows. Living in the cave makes me see how hard it is for them. Maybe the men and I have had a difficult time in the camp, but in a different way. Our baggage is depleted, but we have enjoyed the security of the prospect – or the hope, at least – of a return to the outside world. Anna and the children do not have that luxury.

While I started testing different concoctions to replace ink, I began to devise a plan. I tried to write with a mixture made up of soot, ground charcoal and water, but the text spread under my hand. Then

I had the idea of blending soot with blood I drew from a hare, with Nikolai's help. The blood soon smelt nauseating and I did not seem to be able to draw it without help, so I returned to a mixture of soot and water. I do not know if these notes will survive, because some of the text gets smudged as soon as the sheets press against each other. I have become so used to the idea of recording memories and information that the thought of losing my notes oppresses me disproportionately. I came up with the idea of sprinkling sand over the writing, hoping that it would help preserve my entries.

Agolasky would surely have been pleased that the writing on the preserved pages of his diary, though smudged in places, was still legible. Time has not faded it. Only pages that have got wet have become an even grey, without any real text, just the odd letter discernible here and there.

Finally I have made my decision and summoned up my courage –

– Anna's eyes are dry, her face determined.

– I took my leave of them. I cried as I stumbled towards the forest, away from the cave –

Have I forgotten the camp deliberately, so I would not find my way back?

Today it is raining. I am wet – I caught a squir –
Sle –

I am cold –

– I am close –

OCTOBER IN THE YEAR 1822

I arrived at the edge of the camp today. I remained hidden in the forest to observe the situation. The camp appears suspiciously quiet. The fire in front of the shelter is dead, but the equipment is still there; the men have not yet left. I kept watch for a fairly long time but saw nobody. I drew back, hid carefully in the middle of a heap of rocks and remained there, thinking.

I have been hiding for a good while now. Dusk has fallen. It gets dark so early that I am sure we are now in October. The camp remains dark. No light burns in Moltique's cabin. I wonder if the professor is dead or alive.

It is morning again.

I am hungry and have run out of water. I suck at the cured meat Anna wrapped up for me and lick leaves wet from the night. They taste of soil. I am cold, too. I try to stay inside the elk skin I got from the cave but I am still frozen. Shivers shake my malnourished body. I should start moving briskly to get the blood circulating in my veins, but I dare not move more than the distance between these two heaps of rocks, one closer to the camp than the other.

I am back at my observation post near the camp. I saw that some of the dogs are still in the camp. No sign of the men, though, and there is no discernible movement in Moltique's quarters. The dogs seem in good condition; I do not think they have been by themselves for long. They are tied up with a long string and I see them visiting their trough to eat and drink. One of them is the leader and I notice it lifting its head every now and then, looking towards my hideaway. It recognizes me, though, and does not feel the need to warn the camp of my presence.

Han –

Han –

Only a moment ago, my hands were trembling so badly I could not write. Now I am a little calmer.

The men are still in the camp. One of them, Balls, walked right past my hiding place. He stopped and I sensed he had heard something out of the ordinary. I breathed heavily. I tried to hold my breath, but it only made the situation worse. I nearly choked. When Balls finally gave up and left, I gasped for air, like a fish out of water. The constriction gripping my lungs was hard to shake off. Even now, I am inhaling slowly just because I can.

Today, I saw Balls sitting in the camp by the dogs. He was shaving off slices of cured meat, putting them in his mouth, even giving the odd one to a dog. He is close to the dog, I know. I saw him babbling nonsense to it, giving it a scratch. The dog tolerated his caressing patiently, staring at my hideaway and moving its brows. No living being could have looked more worried. Even Balls seemed finally to notice. He bent towards the dog, followed its gaze and fixed his own on the heap of stones. I tried to lie as low as possible.

Finally, Balls put the knife into the sheath, got up and scratched the enormous frontage to which his nickname corresponded, never removing his gaze from my hiding place. When he turned and began trudging to the cabin, I decided to take to my feet.

It was fortunate I did, because Balls came back to my hideaway shortly after, pointing a gun. I saw him eyeing the ground suspiciously; I had, no doubt, left numerous prints behind me. Luckily, I had aroused only Balls's suspicion; if it had been Bruno, I would not be here writing about these events. That hunter genius would have tracked me down in an instant and I would have been speared and skinned like a pig.

It snowed today. Frail stars danced slowly down. Each one thawed upon hitting the ground; the small, perfect points became water and vanished, dream-like. Those beautiful, innocent, disappearing flowers were a sign of approaching winter. Soon I would be at the mercy of snow and ice, lacking tent, kit and the support of the men. Winter in this region is severe; gales and blizzards ice the landscape, freezing it to death for months, and if not the cold then the dark will crush a man. I am ready to die. I mourn only my father, my mother, my dog – and Anna. None of them would ever learn my fate.

I fell asleep and was woken by dried tears stinging my cheeks.

I do not know what to do. I have no plan.

I am hungry, I am weak. Forgive me, Father, my stupid courage; I should not have enlisted for this journey. Forgive me, Anna, my feebleness; I cannot do anything for you or the children. Forgive me.

I am useless, Superfluous. Pitiful. I am ashamed of myself. I would like to put an end to this wretch, this shrivelling body, but I am not capable of that, either.

MOLTIQUE LIVES! HE LIVES!

Moltique looks miserable; a bent cripple, a raving lunatic. He is… He.

I have calmed down. The Moltique who interviewed, selected and recruited me for this expedition was respected, intelligent, mysterious, courageous and aware of his own worth. During the journey, I discovered his other side – the unscrupulous and cruel one. He is only a man, after all. A vulnerable human being. A wreck; if that, even. A man reduced to a shell. I watch him dragging himself round the camp and grieve. I cannot put my feelings into words.

Futile. How futile.

Now I see Cook and Fist! They have shrunk. Even Fist. Was my memory of them false? Did I think they were bigger? More dangerous? Stronger? Faster? They look older and more tired than when I last saw them. They withdraw frequently from the other men, appearing to engage in some kind of consultation. What are they planning? What stops them from going? Is it really me they want to find, not their lives somewhere far away from the camp?

I do understand. They want their journey to yield a reward. They want the children. They believe the children will make them rich. They go on trying because they have nothing to lose.

I must not get caught. There is a risk that Anna and the children will try to rescue me – and that is what Cook and Fist want.

I moved further from the camp yesterday – today? – towards the brook. I ate a small fish. It was bony and cold, but I forced it down my throat. I do not know how long I shall survive. The winter? Unlikely. My life is measured in days… Stop it, I say to myself. Pull yourself together! I attempt to stand up but my shoulders slump. I am finished.

I have to try: I want to rescue the mad professor and flee the camp. What do I owe Moltique? My respectability.

Today I crept back to my hiding place. I settle behind the rocks and try to establish a link to the God my father taught me to know. I do not hear him. Instead, I sense Anna's presence. It worries me. I do not see the children anywhere, but I know how skilled they are at hiding. If they have come for my sake, I hope they are quicker and craftier than Cook and Fist. Could they help me?

I thought I was used to fear. I fear more than ever. Too much to lose, and yet nothing. Life is a lightweight currency in the exchange that also deals in Death.

Anna, I whisper your name. Not a sound.

Iax, you reply. Not a sound.

I can no longer wait. I will do it today. Farewell.

The last text of the camp notes is published in the form the committee believes Agolasky intended. In the original entry, the lines are shaky, the words barely legible. But these may be Agolasky's intended words:

The men turn like cotton reels in a massive net which glimmers among the trees. Their bodies are as light as beehives, their mouths open. Nobody hears their screams. This sacrifice will not bring back Nikolai, or Durak, or Katya or Roberto the Lion King. They were brave and quick but unarmed. Anna is not among the dead. My joy at that is small but bright.

OCTOBER 15TH IN THE YEAR 1868

'It snowed today. Frail stars danced slowly down.
Each one thawed upon hitting the ground; the
small, perfect points became water and vanished,
dream-like. Those beautiful, innocent, disappearing
flowers were a sign of approaching winter.'

I wrote those lines and so I may use them again.
Today is exactly like that day almost fifty years ago:
the sky is covered in a grey-blue mass of cloud and
the first snowflakes are floating gently down onto
the autumnal landscape. My eyesight has grown
poor, but with my magnifying glass, I observe the
heavenly artist's aspiration at symmetrical perfec-
tion. The wisp of snowy lace stays on the creeper's
red leaves for just a short while before disappearing, leaving barely a drop of itself. Was it real or a
dream? Sheer madness? There, in front of my eyes,
or nowhere? What is such a thing? Nothing? My
notes are welcome to disintegrate as futile verbiage.
I do not see my Anna in them, nor the children.
A series of horrific images lives in my head, but I
cannot get hold of them. Did they happen to me or
did I imagine everything?

This is what happens to me more and more often:
anything can take my mind back to the forest, to
Anna and the children. Did I invent them? My
missing finger is proof of my participation in the
Expedition of All Time, as our journey was dubbed
following our return:

> *In 1819, around ten men joined the Expedition
> of All Time, led by Professor Moltique, who*

*was known for his sensational discoveries. Their
aim was to find the heirs of Paphlagonia. Two
of them have come back, the professor and his
young assistant, Iax Agolasky, a Russian with
fluent French. But what happened to the men
travelling with them – or the young reporter
Oliver Alleg, an enthusiast of the ravings of
Jean-Baptiste Lamarck, who is said to have gone
to track down what strange things breed in the
forests of north-west Russia. Is it a curse, God's
sign to us to leave alone what He decrees?*

*Moltique's representatives have informed us
that the professor does not give statements to
the press. He is resting in a private sanatorium
in Switzerland after his demanding journey and
will return to his work commitments in due
course. Iax Agolasky, in turn, claims to be unable
to report on the details of the secret expedition
without the professor's permission.*

I was pretty imaginative. They left me alone. The
press wrote about our journey for a time, unearth-
ing all Moltique's indisputable achievements, as
well as his questionable ones, at the same time
presenting arguments for and against the existence
of the children of shadows. The academy did not
comment; those in Parisian scientific circles did
not want to become a laughing stock. I assume
one of the decision-makers met Moltique and saw
what I saw – euphemistically put, the professor
was not well. Finally, people lost interest. Moltique
was left alone in his sanatorium. Oliver Alleg
vanished without a trace. Or that was the general
assumption.

I visited the professor in 1832, once I had saved enough money for the trip from my teaching. Moltique was incarcerated in a private sanatorium on the outskirts of a small village in the Alps. Somewhat by chance, I learned that his relatives did not want to have anything to do with him. The reason became clear to me in the sanatorium. The conceited, nasty professor had become a conceited, nasty lunatic, who wallowed in his own excrement and was afraid of animals – spiders in particular. My visit was fairly brief, I have to admit. When he saw me, his demented eyes lit up strangely and he pushed himself up from the wheelchair with his strong arms, shouting, 'Are you the one who controls them, those creatures from the other side?' Then he spat at me, shouted insults and made hand signals – I did not understand all of them. I turned round, descended to the village, ordered a hot toddy and decided to forget Moltique and the whole trip.

Only, I couldn't.

They returned to my mind day and night. They still do. When I look at the pictures I have created, likenesses of the children I think I knew, I feel despair – a despair that has oppressed me for years. I will never find out if they really existed – and if they did, what happened to them. I have not tried to produce an image of Anna. Nobody in this world resembles her. Those forest-coloured eyes, hair the colour of a pine, small strong frame – courage, strength, wisdom. She is mine. My secret. Yearning is like a stick pushed from heart to brain. A torment, an ache. Was man created to bear such burdens?

Ten years ago, in 1859, an Englishman called Charles Darwin published a work called *The Origin of Species*, in which he posited that all types of beings, including man, descended from other creatures. Moltique tried to argue something similar on our expedition – before he got distracted by theories about werewolves. I recall wondering if Moltique was still alive and what he might be thinking of the attention Darwin was attracting. Moltique himself would have enjoyed the limelight. Caricatures or slander would not have troubled him, as long as they were drawing everyone's gaze towards him.

I was not overly interested in Darwin and the uproar to which he gave rise. Instead, I happened to see a small news item about a man who exploited the publicity Darwin was getting to sell stories about some children who were half-human and half-animal living in a forest – he claimed to have sighted these creatures himself. I thought it might be Oliver Alleg. But I never found this mystery man and my suspicions were never confirmed. Bitter disappointment burned a hole in my soul. All the same, I am sure that Alleg found Anna and the children. Did he talk to them? What happened? Did he lose his wits in the solitude of the wilderness like Moltique – or did he meet the same fate as the men? I never found out, and now I never shall. I shall take my ignorance and pain to the grave with me. I shall not leave a descendant behind to carry the same trait as my mother – may she rest in peace – and I am proud of that, though I have been forced to disappoint Rosa with my anti-child sentiment.

I have led a life filled with denial and lonely questions.

Why did I not return to the cave myself, then? I did not know how. I had no idea where it was and how to get there. Nobody at the academy would receive me – and when I persisted in trying to gain admission, a group of men, fairly similar to Moltique's gang, beat me up one night on my way home. To Rosa I claimed they were a bunch of drunkards. She tended to my contusions patiently, but with suspicion in her eyes.

I found myself in a cul-de-sac. My life was a sea of flames isolated by high walls.

Without Rosa, I would have gone mad. My efficient, capable, sensible, laughing, strong Rosa, my life on the brink of death. Rosa, if you ever read my diary, know this: in this life I have loved and love only you. In a parallel reality, somewhere over there, my heart belongs to Anna.

Somewhere over there, soon. Shall we meet?

Iax Agolasky died five days after completing his final diary entry, in his childhood home in St Petersburg. His wife, Rosa Dolores Agolasky, and their adopted daughter, Florence, were at his deathbed. In a letter she wrote the next day, Rosa told her sister Olivia about Iax's passing:

> *I'm moving to Paris; yesterday, Iax fell into eternal sleep. Florence, myself and the children of shadows – as he called his favourite photographs – were by his bedside. You remember the photographs he created, enlisting villagers and dressing them so they were half-animal, half-human?*
>
> *I suppose he was considered rather unhinged, but photography was his sole obsession.*
>
> *'Do you want to depict things? This is the most precise way there is. Drawing, bah! Words, bah, bah, bah!' So he would hector me. How angry he was if I described things half-heartedly, vaguely! 'Brown or grey?' he might demand if I described, say, a bird I had seen. Words were inadequate in his eyes: 'You make mistakes with them; they demand too much from their users. And you can lie with them; claim a beautiful object is ugly and a dirty one is clean.'*
>
> *Without Félix Tournachon, the master photographer I told you about, he would surely have gone totally mad. Thanks to Nadar, he was able to take pictures with light in his final years. There is – was – much that was bewildering and*

unusual about Iax; one such thing is that he insists – insisted. This is hard: how do I put him into the past tense when I still feel his hand on mine?

But yes, he was adamant that he invented photography, only as an idea, on that strange expedition he went on as a young man. Sometimes I feel that understanding that excursion would have been the key to his soul. He is – was, was! – somehow pained and driven in his documentation. His diaries! There are many. I don't intend to read them. I will allow his soul to rest in peace; my own, perhaps, too. In this life I have loved and only love him, my Iax. In a parallel reality, somewhere over there, he is no longer mine.

Olivia, can you believe I'm writing this? Now I must weep.

Acknowledgements and Postscript

Following the expedition, Iax Agolasky stopped working at the academy. First he became a teacher, then he found work at a small art gallery, where he met his future wife, Rosa Dolores Drulane. They married in 1839. While having his twentieth wedding anniversary photograph taken by Gaspard-Félix Tournachon in 1859, Iax again became interested in this new form of documentation, which matched the visions he saw in the forest. Tournachon (1820–1910), known as Nadar, was a French photographer, cartoonist, author and hot-air balloonist. A pioneer of portraits, Nadar published numerous photographs of his contemporaries, including Guy de Maupassant and Sarah Bernhardt, and also made friends with his subjects.

Despite the age difference, Iax and Nadar shared several interests and had a similar sense of humour. Iax benefited from Nadar's good advice and soon built his own camera, testing different exposure and printing methods. In 1866, Iax became seriously ill. This did not prevent him from working hard on the children's photographs, using cyanotype, a cheap and simple technique.

Iax died, broken by a long illness, in 1868. The fate of the negatives following his death is unknown. Mrs Rosa Dolores Agolasky lived on her own after her husband's demise and passed away in 1870.

I thank the photographer Pekka Nikrus for acquainting me with Moltique and Iax Agolasky, via an exhibition of his work. I wanted to give the children a voice. Instead, I found myself in a forest in north-west Russia, getting to know Iax himself, rather than the children. We share a burning desire to remember, and to remind future generations of our existence. During our joint expedition, I understood that, however hard we try to capture our experiences, we still cannot be totally sure about what is real and what is illusionary. And when we die, we take our fleeting sorrows and joys with us, quite as if they had never existed, as if we were mere illusion ourselves. There is something consoling and, at the same time, melancholy about the thought. Iax, is that what you wanted me to convey through your story?

—VIRVE SAMMALKORPI

Subscribe

Discover the best of contemporary European literature: subscribe to Peirene Press and receive a world-class novella from us three times a year, direct to your door. The books are sent out six weeks before they are available in bookshops and online.

Your subscription will allow us to plan ahead with confidence and help us to continue to introduce English readers to the joy of new foreign literature for many years to come.

'A class act.' GUARDIAN

'Two-hour books to be devoured in a single sitting: literary cinema for those fatigued by film.'
TIMES LITERARY SUPPLEMENT

A one year subscription costs £35 (3 books, free p&p for UK)

Please sign up via our online shop at www.peirenepress.com/shop

BASMEH & ZEITOONEH
RELIEF & DEVELOPMENT

Peirene is proud to support Basmeh & Zeitooneh.

Basmeh & Zeitooneh (The Smile & The Olive) is
a Lebanese-registered NGO. It was established in
2012 in response to the Syrian refugee crisis.
B&Z aims to create opportunities for refugees to
move beyond being victims of conflict and help
them to become empowered individuals who one
day will return to their own country to rebuild
their society. Today the organization is managing
nine community centres in the region: seven in
Lebanon and two in Turkey.

Peirene will donate 50p from the sale of this book
to the charity. Thank you for buying this book.

www.basmeh-zeitooneh.org